Once Upon a Time

Serendipity, Indiana - Book Eight

by

Magdalena Scott

Paperback Release July 2017

ISBN-10:0-9971922-3-2

ISBN-13:978-0-9971922-3-0

Cover Art by Elusive Dreams Designs

Stock Art from DepositPhotos.com

Published by Jewel Box Books

THE STANDISH FAMILY
OF SERENDIPITY, INDIANA

Lillian Standish—Family matriarch; widow of **Harry**; recently retired from running the family Christmas tree farm, and tiny cabin bed and breakfast.

Lillian and Harry's children in order of age are:

Jim Standish—Oldest son; his law office is in town, but he also works on the Christmas tree farm. Married to **Melissa, aka Mel (Singer)**, who is a realtor. Jim and Melissa have the lead roles in SMALL TOWN CHRISTMAS and CHRISTMAS WEDDING. They reside on the tree farm with their son, **Matthew**.

Carla (Standish) Barnett—Dress designer to the stars. Her shop, Creations, is on the Serendipity town square, but her clientele is international. She has a house on the tree farm, which she now shares with husband **Jared** and his children, **Katie** and **Miles**. Carla and Jared star in THE RING.

David Standish—Travels each week for his career, but is home at the farm on weekends. Takes off annually from Thanksgiving through Christmas to devote full-time work to the family business. He and wife **Emily (Kincaid)** are the parents of **Isabel**, the first child to unite the Standish and Markland families. David and Emily star in EMILY'S DREAMS.

Francie (Standish) Carrington—Moved back to Serendipity to take over the running of the tree farm. THE ROAD NOT TAKEN is about Francie and her husband **Brad**. They have an adult son, **Joseph**.

Not a family member, but a dear friend—**Alice Williams** appears in books one through six. THE BLANK BOOK is the love story between Alice and movie star **Robert Diamond**.

THE MARKLAND FAMILY OF SERENDIPITY, INDIANA

Reba Markland is the widow of **Geoffrey**. She has a large supporting role in EMILY'S DREAMS, and is an important player in A PIECE OF HER SOUL. She also appears in other Serendipity books.

Reba and Geoffrey have two daughters, Jennifer and Jacqueline.

Jennifer (Markland) Kincaid runs the consignment shop, EMILY'S DREAMS, and is married to **Marcus Kincaid**. They have four children:

Emily (Kincaid) Standish is married to **David Standish** (EMILY'S DREAMS). They have a young daughter, **Isabel**.

Ben Kincaid lives and works on the west coast.

Taylor and Hannah Kincaid (twins). Taylor's story is ONCE UPON A TIME, and Hannah will star in A COWBOY FOR CHRISTMAS, coming in Autumn 2017.

Jacqueline Markland (now Marshall), Jennifer's sister and Reba's daughter, returned to Serendipity after a long absence, and is the star of A PIECE OF HER SOUL.

PROLOGUE

HERE'S WHAT YOU need to know about me. I've always been a realist. I never believed in love at first sight, fate, or serendipity.

Well, except for the Serendipity I was raised in—that's the name of my hometown in the quiet, rolling hills of Southern Indiana.

But that mumbo jumbo people say, like, *It was a match made in Heaven.* Or *It* was *meant to be.* Seriously. I wouldn't get sucked into that kind of thinking.

The only kind of woo-woo I knew about first-hand was the twin kind, and that's DNA or something really boring and scientific, right? I know twin *coincidences* are real, because my identical twin sister Hannah and I have lived plenty of them.

But what I didn't realize was, I'd be permanently changed by what happened on that cold, rainy day when

Hannah and I were twelve years old. We were being punished for something—I don't remember what, but knowing the way we were back then, I'm sure it was well deserved—and had no screen time. Phones and laptops were confiscated, and we had the day to nurse our anger, stuck together in the room we shared.

But we slipped up to the attic, moving silently, so we didn't get into even more trouble.

That day Hannah and I were on a mission to find something to entertain us. Of course there weren't any tech items, but in our desperation, we were just looking for something different. The attic was stuffed full of old furniture, cartons of Christmas decorations, and loads of other boxes, some of which weren't labeled. Hey, it was better than sitting in our room staring at each other, or trying to re-read the books and magazines we had.

I saw it first—an old trunk sort of wedged back under the eaves, mostly hidden by boxes of who-knows-what. I started to dismantle the wall of stuff, to reach it. "I've never noticed this up here before."

Hannah peered at the trunk before pitching in. "Me either."

Once we'd created space to access it, she tried to open the heavy metal latch. I moved piles of old magazines

2

and catalogs off the top, onto an empty spot on the floor. I hit my head on the steeply slanted eave when I stood up.

She glared at me. "Watch it, Taylor. We're trying to be quiet, remember?"

I rubbed my head, which hurt like crazy. "Thanks for your concern."

Down on my knees next to her, I looked for something to pry up the lid, and finally found a paint scraper. "Who knows how long this thing has sat here." I worked for a bit before the top suddenly flew upward. I was quick enough to catch it before it, too, got whacked on the wooden roof brace, announcing to Mom that we were in the attic.

The wedding dress was on top, folded between layers of tissue paper. I picked it up and the thing unfurled, the weight of the heavy satin sliding out and down with a soft, sighing *whoosh.*

Hannah reached out a hand and smoothed it down the skirt. "Wow. It's beautiful." She got busy with the trunk, digging out a pair of white leather slippers with low heels.

Then she picked up a thin, leather-bound book. "Whoa. Check this out. There's a bunch of them in here." She flipped open the one in her hands, and her eyes widened. "Diary. We've got somebody's diaries here, Taylor."

I read the precise handwriting. "Her name was

Opal."

I was awash in cold chill, holding the dress, watching Hannah. Her voice seemed to come from the bottom of a deep well. Flashes of scenes flew past while I imagined the girl who owned this dress, and planned her wedding to take place in our backyard, under a big white tent. Not hundreds of people, but still a crowd. Bride's side, groom's side, and one attendant each. The girl's sister was her bridesmaid, wearing a dress of similar cut, but in pale pink. The flowers, the music—provided by someone in the house playing piano—and the windows open so the sound wafted out to the guests.

The yard I imagined was much bigger than ours, because there weren't other houses around. Just our house, the lawn, and beyond that, acres of fields.

Then I was being shaken, pulled away from the wedding scene.

"Taylor," Hannah hissed, staring into my eyes from inches away. "Wake up or I'll slap you."

I blinked, remembered where we were and what we were doing, and took a deep breath. I carefully folded the dress back and Hannah helped me return it to the layers of tissue.

"You know," I said, "maybe Mom's right about us

spending too much time online. I just had the weirdest dream, standing here."

Hannah laughed softly. "Excellent. Now we have the perfect way to spend our punishment time. Come up here and go through all the un-labeled boxes. It's almost as good as reality TV.

But we never found anything else in the attic that held our interest, or excited our imaginations, like the contents of the trunk.

The trunk was our secret for a long time. For Hannah it was entertaining, but for me it was more than that. It wasn't until years later that I realized how much more.

CHAPTER ONE

HANNAH AND I had packed our stuff. Mom drove her van, and Dad his pickup, to help us haul everything from our college dorm in Bloomington back to Serendipity.

Good-bye, Indiana University, awesome seat of learning and partying. Leaving was sad on so many levels.

Hannah was driving our jam-packed Ford Focus, following Mom and Dad along Highway 37 south. "I'm not staying a single day longer than I have to," she said, referring to moving back in with our parents.

We'd had this conversation plenty of times in recent weeks, as the job offers continued to *not* pour in. But we still needed to reassure each other that we weren't taking a giant step backward. "I know," I said. "Moving home makes good sense for now, though."

Going home to Serendipity seemed our only option. We both loved Bloomington and would have enjoyed staying there. But without decent paying jobs, we couldn't afford it. We both had polished our online resumes, and our Linked In profiles were sparkled to the max. We should be heading in a completely different direction at this moment. Toward our future, instead of toward our stupid, boring past.

Hannah glanced at me. "Is something wrong with us, Taylor?"

I knew what she meant. Most of our friends had found jobs in their fields. She and I weren't top in our class—we had spent plenty of time partying after all, not to waste that opportunity. But we'd had decent grades, were intelligent, and quick learners, if someone would give us a chance. Her degree was in Environmental Management, and mine was Marketing.

"We'll be snapped up any day now," I assured her, with more certainty than I had. "Meanwhile, we live in our old rooms at home for free, and take a break. We've worked hard, and we deserve a vacation before we sign on for the jobs of our dreams."

Hannah changed lanes, following Mom around a slow RV on the divided highway. "How much of a vacation can it be, when we're stuck in Serendipity with no money and nothing to do?"

We rode in silence quite a while, each picturing how awful it would be. Serendipity, Indiana, population about six thousand boring people, had little to offer anyone our age. The nearest entertainment was the Louisville, Kentucky area, just under an hour away. Plenty of movie theaters, shopping, restaurants, and bars there, all of which required money.

"I don't have much cash left after we filled the gas tank today," Hannah said—a statement she had already made when we were at the gas station.

I had a few dollars, and next time we filled up, it would be on me. Good thing we wouldn't be driving much. "I know. I know."

Hannah adjusted the car's interior temperature down, as hers started to rise. "Dad wasn't very receptive about continuing our allowance. His reaction, when I asked, was a cross between blowing up mad and laughing in my face."

I had seen it, and had been glad *she* asked him so I didn't need to. "Did you see Mom's face? Oh, maybe not since we were all loading stuff. She just turned her back and kept working, shaking her head and not standing up for us."

"Maybe they're having money trouble," Hannah said. "Surely they're not still paying off bills from Emily's wreck?"

I looked, unseeing, out the side window. Occasional homes or barns, and plenty of fields, sped by. "Her hospitalization and then the rehab. And then her *wedding*. Our big sister has cost the parents a bundle, I bet."

"Well, it's not like her wedding was a big event. But yeah, that wreck had to hit them hard, right in the bank account. We can't say anything to them about it, though. They're always so, *We're lucky she didn't die, and look how great she's doing now.*

We started up another gentle hill, and I held up my phone trying to get a signal in spite of the limestone cut the highway ran through. "Right. Of course, we're all glad she didn't die. But the way they make such a big deal of her, now she's turned into almost a different person. It's like they've forgotten how much of a pain she was before the wreck, all the terrible choices she made."

We'd been through this too many times. We wouldn't be able to change our parents' reaction to what had happened, yet we kept struggling to accept it.

Hannah groaned. "I know. They've forgiven her, like nothing ever happened. Ben was the perfect one, but now he's just the forgotten middle kid. And we're being punished unfairly because of the two of them." Hannah smacked her hand on the steering wheel, honking the horn by accident. She giggled. "Anyway, let's not unpack all our stuff. We'll get some good karma going about jobs coming through, by being ready to pick up and head wherever our careers take us."

When we reached Serendipity, the speed limit dropped to thirty, and there was a glut of traffic. I groaned. "Stupid town never changes. Everybody busy going nowhere."

We passed the small houses, small businesses, a bank, and at the stoplight, could see the castle-like courthouse a few blocks away, to our right. Then we picked up speed again on the other side of town, and ten minutes later pulled into the driveway of the two-story white clapboard house we had grown up in.

We got out, stretched, and prepared for unloading. Mom, balancing a tote bag on one shoulder, and a cardboard box in the other hand, tried to unlock the back door. "You girls hungry? I have leftover chili, and can whip up some cornbread."

Dad took the box from her, and unlocked the door, pushing it open with a foot, and letting her go in first. He pierced each of us with a look. "I don't suppose it occurred to either of you to help your mother when she was overloaded."

Hannah and I shrugged in unison.

"It's not our fault if she's carrying more than she can

handle," I said defensively.

One dark brow rose. "Are you sure about that?"

CHAPTER TWO

EMILY BROUGHT DINNER over, so the leftover chili would be tomorrow night's dinner instead. She'd made a ham and potato casserole that had become her famous pitch-in dinner contribution, and a huge tossed salad. I had to admit it felt good for all of us to sit around the family dining table.

All the places were full, but in our brother Ben's spot was Emily's daughter Isabel, in a high chair that had been relegated to the attic since Hannah and I outgrew the need. The second one didn't match because one was bought for Emily, Ben used it, and when we came along, Gran or somebody latched onto a second-hand high chair. I wouldn't want everybody to know that my family were cheapskates. They prefer to use the word *thrifty*, or something equally bogus. My opinion was, if you can't afford to do something right, don't do it at all.

Isabel was a busy, and somewhat messy eater. Emily kept up with her, so Mom wouldn't have a disaster to clean up later. Our niece's brown hair and brown eyes were bouncing the whole time. Almost took my mind off the mismatched high chairs, and the daydream that my house, when I got one, would be perfect. Big, new, and in the right subdivision. Filled with all new furniture that made a statement when people saw it.

The statement would be, Look at me. I'm successful, and my life is going according to my excellent plan.

Hannah nudged me in the ribs, and spoke in a hiss. "Wake up. Conversation alert." The look in her eyes told me the conversation wasn't all that pleasant. Scanning the faces around the table, I knew someone had asked me a question.

"Oops. Sorry. I was watching Isabel, and kinda zoned out. What did I miss?"

Hannah shook her head, and Mom smiled her indulgent smile. Dad set down his fork, looking as if his patience was nearing its limits. "I asked you girls what your plans are. Hannah said you've talked about it, and I'd appreciate specifics. You'll remember I told you that when you graduated, the gravy train wasn't leaving the station anymore."

Dad and his analogies. "I do remember that, Dad, but since I didn't know what the heck you were talking about, I haven't—*we* haven't—dwelled on it."

13

Emily chuckled, took a bite maybe to keep from commenting, and watched Isabel's progress with a bit of casserole on a spoon. The too-large bite dropped and landed on the flowered plastic plate.

I clapped my hands. "Good save, Isabel." Maybe everyone would focus on her instead. *Center stage is yours, girl,* I cheered silently.

"We're waiting," Dad said.

Hannah kicked me under the table in a subtle hint that I needed to take over. I may have flinched.

The plan started to form in my mind. Enough to shut down the inquisition, I hoped, but nothing to raise expectations that we were going to stay, long-term, in Serendipity. "Well, we thought for now, we could help Mom, right? Work at the consignment shop, clean the house and stuff." That sounded respectable, and also like we'd have plenty of free time.

Mom put a hand on mine. "That's sweet, but Emily's Dreams doesn't need more employees. I'm happy doing it on my own. And more importantly, Darlene is happy."

It was a mystery to me that Mom could work for Aunt Darlene without wanting to shove her under a bus. Mom once said that people usually take a while to warm up to Aunt Darlene. So far it hasn't happened for me, and I've known her my whole life. Spending more than five minutes in a room with the kids she and Uncle Jamison raised—our first cousins—sometimes made me want to jump under a bus.

"Mom's even sold some of the stuff up in the attic," Emily said. "It's looking a lot better up there."

My breath caught for a moment, before I reminded myself that the trunk was safely in my room. I'd seen it there when dumping bags and boxes onto the floor.

"I don't know why you don't change the shop name," Hannah said. We had mentioned this a bunch of times, with the same result, like now...

Mom answered, "Darlene likes the name, and she owns it, after all. I like it, too. Such a lovely reminder, each time I put a customer's purchase into one of our logo bags. A reminder of the miracle our Emily is."

Puh-lease. We are eating here.

Emily laughed. "Mom, you're going to give the twins a complex. They're miracles too, right? And Ben?"

Mom's face lit. "Well, of course they are. Each child is a miracle. Thank goodness we have four healthy children, and our beautiful, healthy granddaughter. No more car wrecks, ever. Okay?"

Dad pushed his empty plate toward the center of the table. "I'm sure we can all agree to that. But back to the topic at hand. Your plans, girls? Besides helping your mother around the house, which is a given."

Hannah's face flushed. "Well, Emily? Need help at the Christmas tree farm? It's not exactly using my degree, but in a way it's environmental management, I guess. Maybe I could add it to my resume."

It was my turn to kick her, and I did, maybe too hard, because she jumped. Didn't she realize there was no job on the Standish family Christmas tree farm that either of us would want? Just because Emily had married David Standish didn't mean all the Kincaids were emotionally invested there.

Emily's eyes sparkled, and she seemed to stifle a laugh. "You sure you're interested? Francie runs a *business*. She's not going to keep someone on the payroll who isn't doing their job."

"Well, sure, I guess," Hannah stammered. "I mean, how hard can it be?"

Poor Hannah. She had committed herself. I felt sorry for her—imagined her wandering around the Standish farm, looking for something to do. But we wouldn't be in this predicament long. We both had to keep our spirits up, and remember that our futures were just about to begin.

Someplace else. Someplace *interesting*.

"That sounds a little bit promising," Dad said. "And you, Taylor?"

I forced a smile. The last shreds of our well-deserved break were dissolving into the mostly-empty casserole dish. "I guess I'll go into town tomorrow, and see what lucky business owner will hire me."

I wanted to go to bed and wake up from this small-town nightmare.

Dad's smile was tentative, but I was relieved we weren't being grilled anymore. "At least you both have the beginnings of a plan. And as agreed, you can clear the table now." He pushed back his chair and gestured toward Mom, who was also finished eating.

"Honey, I'm sure the girls are tired," she said.

Dad walked behind her chair, put his hands on her shoulders, and kissed the top of her head. "I'm sure we're *all* tired."

Boy, he was losing the charming George Clooney look all our friends swooned about, and was morphing into the Grinch.

****

Hannah and I cleared the table, put leftovers into the fridge, washed and dried all the dishes, and scrubbed the high chair. Joining us in the kitchen after talking a while longer with Mom and Dad, Emily slid her spotless casserole dish into a carrier and hefted Isabel onto her other hip. "Thanks for washing the dish for me, girls. Good luck tomorrow with the resumes, Taylor." She turned to Hannah. "And I'll see you at the farm tomorrow. Not too early the first day, right? Let's say nine."

Neither of us replied, and the flicker of a wicked grin on Emily's face was brief. Was the whole family against us?

Later, I flopped into Hannah's bean bag chair, the escaping air reminding me of the quick loss of our vacation idea. "Well, *you* really stepped in it with both feet."

She threw herself onto her canopy bed. "You didn't do that much better. At least I know the people I'll be working with. And it's a Christmas tree farm. What can there be to do in May?"

I shuddered. "I don't know, but just the word *farm* makes me think hard work. You know the farm kids in school were always so focused and goal-oriented. Remember that year we were in 4-H, because that cute boy asked us to join? All the other kids had chores at home like crazy, and still did a ton of projects for the county fair."

She covered her eyes with a hand. "Ugh. Yeah, and you and I only turned in one project each, and got that participation sticker. Sucked."

I could still picture the display area when we went to the fair that year. "Ours looked like crap compared to everyone else's."

Hannah's eyes flashed. "I know. And then that boy started going steady with that one chick—can't remember her name—"

"Yeah. I think they got married last year." I knew they had. Their photo was in the local paper and I'd avoided looking at the thousands of others on Facebook. Photos set on the farm, with a tractor, on a stack of hay bales, and so forth. "Back to my original point, I'm just saying you and I may not be farm material."

She raised her head and glared at me. "I have to go tomorrow. I said I would. But while you're out floating resumes, take mine too, okay?" She hopped up, pulled her laptop from its bag and set it on her desk. "I'm gonna make sure it's ready, and print some copies. And I'll check online to see if there are any new job listings I'm interested in."

I climbed out of the beanbag. "Awesome. I'll get the printer set up, and get into my resume too. What a day, huh?

Just when we thought we were gonna catch a break."

"Uh huh." Hannah wasn't listening to me, but focused on her computer.

With a hand on her door knob, I turned back to her. "Whatever jobs we have to settle for now, we'll save every penny toward renting a place in the metro area. We already know the rent is cheaper than Bloomington, and maybe our dream jobs will land us in Louisville. That'd be okay. Not like being in another part of the country, but it's a step."

Hannah looked up at me, her face probably mirroring my own sadness at our turn of events.

We'd gone from being celebrated at graduation, to feeling like moochers. Well, nobody was in more of a hurry than I was for us to get good jobs and start working. That was our ticket out of Serendipity, and away from being pushed around.

Yeah, when we were on our own, we wouldn't have anybody to answer to. It couldn't happen soon enough for me.

In my own room, I got out my laptop and powered it up, set up the wireless printer that Hannah and I shared. I had won the coin toss for the larger room when Emily had to move downstairs after her wreck.

Waiting for my resume to come up, I thought how

different Ben's college graduation had been. We all trooped up to Bloomington together in Mom's van. Even David and Emily. Afterward, we took pictures, squeezed into the best pizza place in town after a horrendous wait, and listened to Ben talk about his future. His stuff from our house, along with what he had accumulated in the house he rented with friends, was packed into a moving pod. It would be waiting for him out west, where he had a job and apartment lined up.

It stunk to have an over-achiever like that as a sibling. The perfect child, Emily had called him for years. First in disgust, but after her rehab, it was more a sign of respect.

So, okay, Ben was doing well, and I didn't begrudge him that. He had worked for it. Emily, in her messed-up way, had taken a crooked path that ended up pretty great. Hannah and I would be fine. Better than fine. In a few months we wouldn't even remember today's disappointments.

I brushed away some stupid tears. I couldn't see the laptop screen through them.

At least Hannah knew where she'd be tomorrow at nine, and even if the job was dull, she'd be surrounded by family and almost-family.

Tomorrow, I had to make the rounds of business

owners in Serendipity, who I hadn't exactly spent a lot of time getting to know, since Hannah and I preferred to drive to the city to do any shopping.

What a homecoming.

CHAPTER THREE

WE STARTED THE morning with an argument about the car.

"I have to drive to the tree farm," Hannah said. "You don't expect me to walk there, do you?"

"If you went across the fields—"

She huffed, chomping a piece of bacon.

Mom looked at me over her coffee mug. "You can ride with me, Taylor, since you're going to town. If you get a job at the factory, you can start riding with your father. That's an early start, though. He leaves by six, you know."

I almost spewed coffee. But she couldn't mean it. Work at the factory? Me?

"I'll go around the square, see what I find." Working a cash register at a shop would be less money, but better hours, than the factory. And considering Dad's attitude yesterday, I wasn't sure he'd let me work there if I wanted to.

****

I rode to the consignment shop, Emily's Dreams, with Mom, and watched her arrange the stuff on shelves, dig a few items from the storage room, and put them on the painted shelves with things of similar nature.

I picked up a delicate glass mug from a punch bowl set. "Who would buy something like this? It's such an outdated thing to own."

Mom shrugged. "I'm constantly amazed at what sells, and what lingers for months. We get groups of out-of-towners because of Chez Gwen." She handed me a too-cute foldout map. "Jared put this together, and all the shop owners have them. But most times when I ask where folks got the map they're clutching, the answer is Chez Gwen. This is an easy way local businesses support each other."

Chez Gwendolyn, situated on the east side of the town square, is the nicest sit-down restaurant in Serendipity. People my age don't go there much, unless they call for carry-out and pick their food up at the back. But the older generation is all about Chez Gwen.

The maps were nice, but how much difference could they make in encouraging people to shop in Serendipity? I didn't want to open the can of worms Hannah and I referred to as *Don't put a big box store in my county, lest I die.* Mom and Dad were in the camp that believed a place like that would kill a bunch of local businesses, turning the square into a sad collection of empty storefronts, and adding more crime. Hannah and I both thought that, with or without a big retailer, the town was on a downhill slide. Another reason to be sure we were out and successful, so it wouldn't affect us.

I hitched my purse onto my shoulder. Mom had insisted I wear the skirt suit she'd bought me for interviews. On a weekday in Serendipity, I felt ridiculous in it. The printed resumes were in manila folders—one for me, one for Hannah—inside my handbag. "I'll get going now. Back in a little while, I guess."

She gave me a hug. "Good luck, honey. I know you'll do great." She'd said the same thing to Hannah when she left, dressed in jeans and an old shirt, and carrying a pair of Mom's rubber gardening boots, *just in case.*

Skipping a bunch of stores, my first stop was on the other side of the square, the dress shop called Creations. Carla Standish was a dress designer whose gowns had appeared at the Academy Awards, Cannes Film Festival, and state dinners in the U.S. and Europe. She was a very big deal. The fact that her shop was in Serendipity was ludicrous, but super cool. If you were lucky enough to have some bucks when Carla had a little wiggle room in her calendar, you could have a Creations original. Carla had recently married the economic development guy Jared Barnett, who had made those shop maps Mom was so enthused about.

The bell over the dress shop door jingled when I entered. An old woman appeared from the back room, smiling. "Good morning. How can I help? Oh—it's Taylor, isn't it?" She cocked her head. "Or Hannah?"

It took me a few seconds to remember why I knew her. She was the old home ec teacher. "Hi, Mrs. Glass. I'm Taylor. I'd forgotten you work here now. No more obnoxious school kids to deal with, right?"

A pained look crossed her face. "I miss teaching, but the administration shut down the home economics department. I was fortunate, and so glad, to be needed here."

Oops. Evidently that career end decision was still a sore spot. Hannah and I had learned how to cook and sew from Mrs. Glass, encouraged by Mom of course. We didn't make our own clothes, but it was good to be able to put a button back on when necessary. Without a doubt, we'd been pains in the backside to Mrs. Glass, as we were to most teachers. Just part of the awesomeness of being identical twins.

I pulled a resume out of my bag. "Mrs. Glass, I'm

looking for a temporary job. Do you know if Carla needs anybody?"

Her look was brief and quickly disappeared, but read something like, *Are you kidding me? Hire you?* Evidently the kindly woman recalled some of my—*our*—classroom antics. She took the paper and smiled as she slid it onto the counter. "I haven't heard Carla say she's looking for more help, but I'll give this to her when she gets back from L.A."

"Wow. L.A., huh?"

"Yes, work and visiting friends."

That probably meant Alice. She married movie star Robert Diamond after a flurry of weirdness about a story she wrote in an old blank book.

"Well, that's cool. When will Carla be back?" I didn't want to get another job if there was a chance of working in the beautiful showroom for a few weeks until I got a call from someplace interesting.

She cocked her head again, a sign she was thinking before speaking. "Late this week. Taylor, are you genuinely interested in eight hours a day at a sewing machine, or with a needle and thread, adding sequins and other hand-applied trim to evening gowns? I don't recall that you were especially interested in sewing."

Busted. "Yeah. Well. I'm not. I thought maybe—" I

gazed meaningfully around the beautiful front room with life size posters of famous women wearing Creations gowns.

She shook her head. "Very little of our time is spent out here, and what is requires knowledge of Carla's work load, the fabrics, cost of each item's production, and of course measuring and fitting. Our days are mostly full of sewing."

I glanced at the resume on the counter. Maybe I'd waste it by leaving it with her. I sort of hated machine sewing, and the tedious sequin thing sounded like torture. "I guess I might not be all that interested."

When I left, the resume was back in my bag. I didn't want to be a seamstress. *Yuck.*

I went to all the offices. Nobody was hiring, but they had paper application forms, and if I wanted to fill those out, they'd put them into their files. If an opening came up, they'd pull out the applications. What an old-fashioned system.

But I picked up two applications at each office. Nobody even wanted to look at the resumes we'd worked so hard on.

It was the same story in the law office, real estate offices, shops, and even Chez Gwen. I didn't want to be a waitress, but knew I had to go into every place, or else my parents would hear that I had been choosy. I also got application forms at city hall and the courthouse, although office staff in both places told me the city and county were under hiring freezes because of budget crunches.

Having finished the last of my route, I trudged along the sidewalk with the last few applications in my hand, since my bag was jammed full. I planned to sit in the back room of the consignment store and fill mine out. I had texted Hannah about the stack of *homework* I was bringing her, but hadn't gotten a response. First, though, I'd stop at the soda fountain for a strengthening milk shake to have at hand.

As I passed the antiques store, the breeze that had been light and warm picked up without warning, and a bunch of the applications flew out of my hand. I let loose with an automatic curse, and chased them, finally rounding them up in the alcove entryway of the antiques store. I collected the papers and straightened, trying to jam them into my handbag, and the door lock clicked. In my peripheral vision I saw the sign being flipped from CLOSED to OPEN.

The courthouse clock chimed, and I glanced at the tower. Eleven in the morning and this store was just opening? That was a great time to start a workday. I made sure the papers weren't too messy, peeking above the top of my bag. Then I smoothed my hair, and gave myself a quick pep talk.

A place full of old stuff, old people. Low key, plenty of time for Facebook. This could work.

When I pushed the heavy door open, I'm pretty sure my shocked surprise was obvious on my face.

CHAPTER FOUR

I KNEW HIM. My brain flashed to a time when his handsome face was suffused with laughter, his eyes full of love.

I blinked, shook my head to clear it. Whoa. I needed that milkshake more than I realized. Low blood sugar was messing with my brain.

He was a handsome devil. I'd heard that old phrase my whole life, but until now never had an understanding of what it might mean.

This guy. A few years older than me, with dark, perfect hair, unsettling vivid green eyes, a narrow face. With broad shoulders, slim hips and long legs, he was dressed entirely in black. The trim-fit long sleeve dress shirt suggested strong arms and torso, the jeans were really black, not faded out gray-ish black. The black leather loafers looked expensive. He wore an expression halfway between a frown and a smile. He was the kind of dangerous-looking man Mom always warned us about, which made him even more intriguing. He sure didn't look like somebody who would be shopping for antiques. Not a man you'd run into on the Serendipity town square, either.

I smiled, stood up straight, making sure my own assets were obvious. With my lousy luck, there was a *Mrs.* Tall-Dark-and-Dangerous in a dusty aisle somewhere.

He flipped on the light switch and took a step back. His arm swept toward the huge shop behind him. "Good morning. Is there anything in particular you're looking for today?"

My eyes dragged themselves from staring at him, and followed his gesture. The place wasn't heaped with dusty shelves, but looked more like the inside of an old house. Small *rooms* were set up as far as I could see. From outside, the building looked massive, and it truly was.

"Oh. So, you're the owner?"

He nodded. "Yes. Ken Abernathy."

I stuck out my hand. "Taylor Kincaid. Mr. Abernathy, I'll get right to the point. I'm looking for a job— a temporary one, because I'm just out of college and nothing in my field has come along yet." I slid one of my resumes out of its folder, pushing aside those pesky application forms from the other places I'd been. He accepted it, his long fingers touching mine.

I felt that touch from the top of my head right through the soles of my stilettos. *Wow.* The man was electric. Somehow I found my voice and spoke, as he frowned in concentration, reading about me.

"Sorry if it's a little bent." Had I managed a light tone, or did I sound desperate? If I didn't get hired here, my next step was Tony's Macaroni and then Al's Place. Fast food was further down the list.

I didn't want to wear a uniform in an unfortunate color, and go home every night smelling like fried food. I remembered how it was when Emily had worked at first one burger joint and then another, being all angry in between about getting fired.

Please hire me. Just for a few weeks so I can have Dad off my back and some money in my purse.

He looked up from the resume, his eyes inquiring but not quite dismissive. "What do you know about antiques?"

The worst possible question. My shoulders slumped, but I raised them again, unwilling to give up. "Absolutely nothing. But I'm a quick learner."

He glanced at the paper again. "A resume usually lists previous work experience, not just education."

My face grew hot. "Right. I know. But I've never had a job. Didn't have time. We were in band and clubs and stuff. Always super busy and—you know—jobs are hard to fit into the few extra hours."

"Is that right? Who is *we*?"

"My twin sister, Hannah and I." My feet weren't thrilled about all this walking and standing in stilettos, and I shifted with nervousness and physical discomfort. I pulled out another copy of my resume and pointed at the appropriate section. "We did a lot of extracurricular stuff, see?"

He wasn't impressed. "No job in college?"

I shook my head, feeling the cozy antique shop slipping away, and promising myself to wear sneakers if I worked in a restaurant.

"And your parents are Marcus and Jennifer?"

A flicker of hope appeared. Small town connections might save me here. "That's right. I rode to town with Mom."

"Your parents have been very good to me since I got to Serendipity. I've worked with them on a community betterment board, and of course your mom is in the Square Shoppes Association, representing Darlene."

Square Shoppes. How accurate on multiple levels.

"My Aunt Darlene has an interior design business in Mendacious, so Mom pretty much runs Emily's Dreams." That was probably true, plus it put another important connection out there in case it would help. "And, you know, Carla up at Creations is almost part of the family. My sister Emily is married to Carla's brother, David Standish."

He shook his head, a slight smile broadening. "And similar connection to my attorney, Jim Standish, his realtor wife, Melissa, and Francie, who runs their family Christmas tree farm."

Hope was burning nicely now. "Yep. Lucky me, right?"

He chuckled. "I get the family connections, Taylor, but I'm not originally from Serendipity."

"Right." As if I didn't know that. I would not have been unaware of this guy.

"Meaning, just because you're the daughter of local business people I have good relationships with, that doesn't make you the ideal employee. The fact that you've never had any kind of job..." He shook his head in disbelief. "No wonder you haven't found something in your field, as you say."

I was heating up now. "Employers want you to have all this work experience, but they don't want to help you get it. You mean you'd give me a chance if I had spent my summers frying burgers? Yet hours of practice, travel, and performances with the band, the flag corps, the cheer squad mean nothing? Do you know how hard any of that is? How many hours of preparation are done behind the scenes before we step out in front of a crowd? That's dedication, you know. I understand hard work that leads up to a show on the football field during halftime when most of the crowd is talking and trooping back and forth to the concession stand, paying zero attention to the awesome band." I sucked in a breath. "Wow—that makes me furious all over again."

"I was going to say something to the effect that working at any job would show work ethic, but you've made an excellent point." He smiled then, the first real smile, and it rocked my world. "So, Taylor Kincaid, welcome to Once Upon a Time. When can you start?"

Once Upon a Time. Though I'd never before set foot inside it, the shop's name always appealed to the little girl in me. The big girl was more impressed with the guy who seemed to run it. I was in for the learning curve of a lifetime about both.

CHAPTER FIVE

AT FIVE-THIRTY, Ken Abernathy locked the door behind me, and I made my way, feet and legs screaming with each step, to the consignment shop.

Mom was standing in the doorway, purse and keys in hand.

"Hey, Mom, can I run in and use the bathroom before we go?"

"Sure, honey, but I was headed straight home."

I guess my face it said it all, because she unlocked the door and we went in. I tried to kick off my shoes, but my feet had swollen, and they weren't going to budge easily. "Be right back."

In the car for the ten minute ride home, Mom's cheeriness, and my physical pain, made me feel like puking.

"So you're working for Ken. I didn't realize you like antiques, honey."

I shot a look at her profile but she didn't seem to be kidding. "I didn't like antiques when this day started, but after working there for a few hours, I can safely say I hate them."

"But—"

"Mom. Come on, it's Serendipity. There aren't dozens of job options, you know. Zero today, except working for good old Ken."

"You don't like him? Honey, you've only just met him, and he did hire you."

Dad was more forceful when the four of us sat at the dinner table. Mom's slow cooker roast and vegetables had never tasted so good. I had to force myself to sit back and breathe once in a while.

Watching me, Dad said, "Taylor, none of us want to hear you whine about working for Ken Abernathy. He gave you a job when you had no experience and no other options. There might be something in fast food, but the hours are unpredictable. At the factory, right now we're at full staff. Not even a job in cleanup, pushing a four-foot mop and emptying trash."

I clenched my mouth shut, so I wouldn't spout off a comment I might regret. Then opened it again, took a bite of potato and carrot. *Yum.* The sandwich, chips, and drink that

Ken had brought me from Chez Gwen were ancient history. My presence meant he didn't have to close down for his lunch meeting at the restaurant, and the meal was a nice surprise. Eating it in the little back room with my feet propped up on a chair was a relief. I had texted Mom and Dad about getting the job, texted Hannah about what a slave driver the handsome Ken turned out to be. The parents congratulated me, and said some over-the-top stuff about my employer.

All I got back from Hannah was *LOL TTYL*.

Hannah, who had eaten even more than I, finally pushed her plate away. "I don't think I can go back tomorrow. Francie said she can do without me."

If I had whined, Hannah had whined times one thousand.

Dad scowled. "Why wouldn't you go to work tomorrow?"

"I need a break. That farm stuff is hard. I'll be too sore to do it again tomorrow."

"Hair of the dog." Dad's voice was a low growl. "You're not skipping a day. You girls don't seem to realize how well these jobs are preparing you for your future."

"Like digging out dead Christmas tree stumps is a step toward a rewarding career in Environmental

Management? Right. *Please*, Dad?"

Dad was hiding a smile behind his water glass. I was sure of it. I'd never known he had such a cruel side. Mom shook her head and got up to start clearing. Dad's eyebrows rose, and Hannah and I lifted ourselves up, and insisted she take it easy since she had fixed dinner. We were glad to clean up.

What had we done to deserve such punishment? But at least cleaning up after dinner wasn't as bad as getting up extra early each day, like Mom did, to get stuff ready for the slow cooker.

After our showers, and in our sleep T's, we hung out in Hannah's room. "Francie is like a drill sergeant," she said. "She's going to turn over the cleaning of the tiny cabins to me. *Yay*. But first I have to prove my work ethic by doing a couple of weeks with the guys who are pulling stumps from last year's cut trees, filling in the holes, and planting new seedlings with little protective cages around them." She stretched, wincing. "It's back breaking even though, to be honest, the stump pulling is mostly done by a machine. The rest, though, is all by hand. And after you plant these seedlings you have to babysit them the whole year, she said—check them for disease, make sure they get water if we haven't had at last an inch of rain in a week."

"Sounds like a science experiment," I muttered, scrolling through Facebook.

"I know, right?" Hannah picked up her phone, and groaned. "Even my wrists hurt. Everything hurts. At least you get to work in a store. Dress up, not look like a vagrant."

"Are you kidding me? I may never be able to wear stilettos again. My feet were screaming so much, I swear I heard them. Our buddy Ken's shop is on three levels, and the only elevator is for moving merchandise. He calls it a big dumb waiter. You raise it from one floor to the other with these thick ropes. Absolutely prehistoric." He'd showed me how to use it. I had the rope burns to remind me.

"When a customer went upstairs, I trailed after them, to help, or watch them. Can you even believe anybody would shoplift an antique?"

Hannah dropped her phone on her bed, laid her head down with a sigh. "People will steal anything, I guess. Some people. But yeah, antiques—I don't get why anybody wants someone else's castoff stuff, free or otherwise."

"The consignment store's success ought to teach you that," I said. "Part of it is not having the bucks to buy new stuff. It creeps me out to think of wearing clothes that somebody else wore. Even though Mom makes sure everything is clean. There's a washer and dryer in the back.

Did you know that?" I had seen it for the first time when I used the bathroom there. "She does laundry at home, and laundry at work too. I don't even understand why she has a job now. She didn't have a job before."

Hannah yawned. "Probably she was bored after we left for college."

"I wouldn't be bored. I'd go shopping, see movies, maybe even hit a museum once in a while. In Louisville, I mean."

"She does stuff with Dad on weekends. I get the idea the two of them are even cozier than they used to be. Did you see them in the dining room when they thought we weren't looking?"

I covered my ears. "Oh, please. No visualizations of our parents' physical relationship."

She held up both hands in defense. "Believe me, not going there. We should be glad their marriage is still good, though. Strong, even. So many of our friends don't have their parents together. It's pretty cool when you think about it."

How did they stay happy when others didn't? Might be something worth paying attention to, if I ever chose to be in a serious relationship.

But for now I had to get to bed, find a comfortable

position, and try to get a good night's sleep. Tomorrow was another long day of antiques, and it was only Tuesday.

CHAPTER SIX

ALTHOUGH KEN'S SHOP opened at eleven, I still had to get up, eat breakfast, and head out with Mom, who opened the consignment store at nine. Without another car, there wasn't an obvious alternative.

"Maybe you could find another way to get to the tree farm," I hinted to Hannah. She glared at me over her orange juice.

"After this supposedly *easy* first week—easy according to Francie and Lillian—I have to be there at eight each day. So don't look to me for sympathy on your early start, sis."

I shivered. Our freshman year in college, we'd had to settle for an eight o'clock class that was required, because all the other sections were full. That whole semester we were late—and cranky.

Hannah slid the last of the scrambled eggs onto her

plate. "You're lucky he opens late though. You can hang out in downtown Serendipity. See the rights. Embrace the culture."

Sometimes I hate being a twin. It was just the sort of thing I'd have said to Hannah if our roles had been reversed.

The only person I could think of that would head to town that time of day was good old Ken.

"So. Mom. What about my boss? D'you think he'd mind picking me up as he heads to town? Really, if its's on his way, that would be in his best interest. I'd be a more cheerful and efficient employee if I got a full night's sleep."

Mom took a slow, thoughtful drink from her thick ceramic coffee mug. "If you want a full night's sleep, go to bed earlier, sweetheart. I know at your age, you girls like to stay up, but there comes a time..." She let the sentence hang, shook her head as if what she'd been saying didn't matter. That was good, because we weren't ready to change lifelong habits. That's why coffee was created. And concealer.

"And I'm a little surprised you don't know where Ken lives," she added.

Hannah giggled. "In Barbie's dream house?"

I snorted coffee, then coughed.

Mom nodded. "Yes. The human sized one. He has an apartment on the third floor of the antiques shop."

"But the store goes up to the third floor. *Oh*—that locked door." Now I felt stupid. All three floors had views to the north, of the courthouse green and the traffic going around the square, but the third floor had a wall of a bunch of old mirrors all over the east side, instead of the stunning view of *cars going north and south on Main Street* that the first two floors had. The wall of mirrors reflected light around the room, which was smaller than the two lower levels.

Hannah whistled. "How creepy. Who would want to live someplace like that? Nobody *normal*."

And I was spending the whole day in this guy's lair? What were my parents thinking?

Mom set her mug down *hard*, and Hannah and I jumped. "There is nothing creepy about living in a spot like that. His great-uncle, that Ken inherited the store from, had the apartment built, and lived there forever. I think, for Serendipity, it's kind of cosmopolitan."

Hannah and I just stared at her. I noticed Hannah's mouth hanging open, so I closed mine. "Okay, Mom. Don't get all defensive, but why didn't you warn me?"

Mom's eyes slid shut for a moment. "You're both quite fond of reminding your father and me that you're grown up and ready to lead your own lives. Getting up in the morning and being at work on time is part of that, you know. Another part is spending time around people who aren't like you. You're in such a hurry to get out of Serendipity, yet when a citizen exhibits the gall to think outside the box, you try to shove them into another one."

She tossed her napkin onto the table. "I'm going to get dinner started. Clean this up before we leave." Mom stomped into the kitchen, while we blinked at each other.

"Why's she so touchy? Hannah asked.

I pushed my chair back. "Dunno. Maybe she's got something hormonal going on. Let's clean this up so we don't catch more grief."

Hannah stacked plates. "You better watch that Ken guy, Taylor. What kind of man moves to Serendipity, takes over an antiques store, and lives upstairs? Sounds vampir-ish to me."

She was just goading me, but I decided to keep a closer eye on Ken. At a minute before eleven, I was at the front door of Once Upon a Time when he unlocked. He looked beat—had dark circles under his eyes. His greeting was mumbled, and he didn't meet my eyes when I walked in. The Vampire Theory occurred to me, and I couldn't hide a grin.

"Back for another day? I wondered." His eyes

traveled all the way to my sneakers. "And wearing comfortable shoes."

I crossed my arms over my chest. It's the only job in town right now, and I'm trying to earn enough money to get out of town. So yeah, I'm back. Thanks.

But out loud I said, "These shoes seemed to make more sense, given the work."

Hannah and I had talked last night. We'd try to save all the money we earned, find a reasonable apartment in the Louisville or across the river, in Jeffersonville or New Albany.

Ken shrugged and stepped back, holding the door until I was in. Closing it, he adjusted the OPEN sign longer than was necessary. I was glad for one thing Mom had said at breakfast—now I understood why Ken was in town. Running an antiques store you inherited wasn't as crazy as paying money for it.

"So, what am I doing today?" I asked.

Ken must have stayed up all night planning work for me. By closing time, I was ready to scream. Whatever he told me to do, I did, but there was never any gratitude. Tomorrow morning I would shop my resume somewhere else—*anywhere*. Ken was really getting on my nerves. The only good thing about this job was the late start.

I washed dust and furniture polish off my hands in the little *Employees Only* powder room at the back of the building that I hadn't noticed the first day. Then I went to the counter where I had stowed my handbag, and retrieved it. I could hear Ken talking. I had forgotten he had a couple of customers upstairs. Five-thirty passed, and I was antsy to get out. Would he pay me for standing here? Doubtful. But I didn't think I should leave without him knowing I was doing so.

I sent Mom a text that I would be there ASAP. Tonight's dinner was a slow cooker version of her famous lasagna. My mouth watered, imagining it. The snack I'd gobbled on my fifteen minute break was ancient history.

A few minutes later, Ken and the two customers came down the creaky stairs, chatting like old friends. Ken looked like a different person when he smiled. More the kind of person I'd like to spend a few hours a day with.

He stepped behind the counter and conducted by far the biggest transaction I'd seen. It would pay me for a couple of months, except, I remembered, I wouldn't be here.

He slid the printed receipt onto the glass counter. "We'll have it all tagged *Sold*. Just give me a call when you're ready for delivery."

The woman put away her credit card, and her

husband shook hands with Ken. "Thanks so much, Ken. We're sure glad we found your store."

"Absolutely." The woman's face glowed with enthusiasm. "We'll be telling all our friends about you. Um—do you have a website? Are you online?"

Ken plucked a business card from the stand created out of a big silver serving spoon. Real silver, I knew, because I had polished it yesterday.

The woman accepted the card and read it, slid it into her bag, and commented on the unusual card holder.

I thought they'd never leave. Ken walked them to the door and said good-bye, then busied himself straightening some things in the window that didn't need attention.

My stomach growled. "Uh, can I leave now? It's late."

"One minute."

Sheesh. I was going to starve at this rate.

Finally he flipped the sign on the door to CLOSED, and turned to me. "You don't shove a customer out the door, Taylor. You take time with them, make sure you do all you can to meet their needs, and make it obvious that they—not just their dollars—are important to you. Makes for good relations and return visits. Plus, like she said, we'll get word of mouth advertising, which is priceless."

I slung my bag onto my shoulder. "Okay, lesson learned. They were some awesome customers, and I'm sure you're glad to have such a big sale. Can I go now?"

He nodded. "Let's open at nine tomorrow. The folks who just left had been here yesterday early. We're lucky they came back."

There went the only perk of the job. "What if somebody comes past at midnight? You going to stay open twenty-four hours?"

I thought he was going to smile, but it turned into a frown. "Time will tell. For now, it's the right time of year to have extended hours. Winter was slow. But since I have help—sort of—this is a good time to experiment. We'll each get a lunch hour. That way, maybe the last hour of each day won't be accompanied by the sound of your stomach growling."

Yikes. He'd heard it? My face got hot, thinking how uncool that was.

He had his hand on the front doorknob, ready to open it for me. "Any reason you can't be here at nine?"

My morning of resume-floating had gone out the window, but I had to be realistic. The only places I hadn't been, I had even less desire to work.

"No. My ride—Mom—gets here before nine. You probably realize that."

He shrugged, not caring. "All right. See you then."

At dinner, Mom said, "You must be doing a really good job for Ken."

Dad nodded. "I don't recall him having even part-time help before."

I don't remember any more conversation, but the lasagna was awesome.

Upstairs, we lounged in my room. Hannah was pleased about Ken changing my hours. "Now you'll understand what it's like to have a real job. That eleven a.m. start was a joke."

I took one of Opal's diaries out of the trunk. "I'm going to save every penny toward our place in the city. You are too, right?"

Hannah looked away, back to the laptop she had been staring at. That was suspicious.

"What are you doing?" I peered over her shoulder before she could move to another tab. "*Horses?* Why are you reading about horses? Is Francie starting a trail ride service through the tree farm?" B&B guests stayed in miniature cabins secluded in the Christmas trees. It was quaint and seriously dull, but the new-ish addition to the farm seemed to be doing really well for the Standish family. Francie was energetic, and since taking over the farm operation from her mom, she'd added a fall festival. So the trail ride idea wasn't unbelievable.

"Won't that be a mess when people swarm all over the farm on foot, in December?" I shivered at the idea of stepping in horse-stuff while looking for a Christmas tree. Or dragging the tree along, and then-*smoosh*.

Hannah slammed her laptop shut. "No, Francie isn't starting trail rides. You don't know everything I'm interested in, Taylor. Just because we're out of school doesn't mean we stop learning about stuff."

Whoa. Somebody was defensive. "I'm just surprised. Didn't know you ever did research that wasn't about celebrities or fashion."

She flipped her hair behind her shoulder. "I'm evolving."

Then I knew. "Okay, who's the guy? Let me guess—somebody who works for Francie commutes on his horse."

Her face was red. "Of course not." She knew it was pointless to try to keep holding me off. We could never keep secrets from each other. In a way it felt like being untrue to ourselves to be less than fully honest with our twin. That was inconvenient sometimes. For Hannah, now was one of those times.

I put the diary back in the trunk, closed the lid. "Spill it. Nobody is going to bed until I hear this story, and it's late already."

"Ugh. You are such a pest."

"I realize that. Same goes, Sis."

She squeezed her eyes shut, as if about to relate something painful. "There's a dude ranch across the road from the tree farm."

"A *what?* Dude ranches are in places like Wyoming, not Indiana."

She nodded. "I know, right? But these people heard of the tree farm and Serendipity. I guess whatever Jared Barnett is doing to advertise the county is working."

"Hard to fathom how Jared picked Serendipity to relocate from Indianapolis," I said. "His poor kids probably hate it here."

Hannah shrugged. "Whatever. Anyway, now that he's the economic development director, he's really working it. So yeah, there's a dude ranch."

"I'm waiting to hear about the guy who works there, riding a horse, looking all studly."

She started to blush. "He doesn't just work there. He

sort of owns it."

This grilling session was the most fun I'd had since graduation day, and I knew she didn't mind. She'd be glad to bare her soul, and then we'd share this little secret. "He *sort of* owns it? What does that mean?"

"It's another family operation. Kind of fits in well because of the Standish farm right there. And they haven't opened to the public yet, but it's really cool, what they have planned. They bought a farm of course, and I guess they're keeping some of the fields in production. Hay and alfalfa to feed the horses, straw for bedding in their stalls. The big, long bunkhouse they built is real rustic looking but is divided up into these hotel-size rooms, each with a private bathroom. Each bathroom is being done in this fake cave-like wall and shower covering. Honoring all the caves in Southern Indiana, you know. The bedrooms have plain wood walls, like a real bunkhouse out west. There's a big fire pit outside the bunkhouse. The guests and guides will tell ghost stories and roast hot dogs and marshmallows there. The chuck wagon, they call it, is a part of the bunkhouse, so if it rains the guests can stay there, around the massive stone fireplace, play board games, talk, read books. And use it for a fire pit if they want, I guess."

I could picture it, but the thought of something so

unique in Serendipity was wild. Not that I'd ever been interested in going to a dude ranch. Unless it had all the comforts of home, and hunky cowboys waiting on me hand and foot. "And a big screen TV in the chuck wagon, right?" I asked.

"No TVs anywhere. Wireless, but that's only accessible in guest rooms. So when people are in the common areas they won't be online."

The dude ranch coolness evaporated. "That's messed up."

She shrugged. "I dunno. It kind of makes sense if people are going there for a vacation, or to get away from the world."

Her face was so lit up, you'd think she had come up with the dude ranch plan herself. "And your guy?"

Her eyes dropped. "Not *my* guy. But how I wish he was. Tall and handsome, with a deep tan and broad shoulders. Eyes that crinkle at the corners when he smiles. And such a gorgeous smile! The whole world just lights up."

I hadn't seen Hannah this animated about a guy since a football player asked her to the prom when we were high school freshmen. "Sister, you've got it bad. What's his name?"

"Jacob Hollingsworth."

"And is this Jacob as crazy about you as you obviously are about him?"

She shook her head, the curtain of strawberry blonde hair preventing a full view of her despair. "To him I'm invisible. His sisters, Jessica and Ashley, were at Francie's for lunch. She's awesome like that, you know. She fixed lunch today, for all of us who were working to meet the Hollingsworths. Big table full of food, out in that building they use as the Christmas shop during the holiday season. After lunch, I guess because I seemed interested, Francie said I could go over with them and look at what they've done on the dude ranch so far. I rode back on one of their four-wheelers."

"Not a horse?"

She glared at me. "They're real considerate, and wouldn't want to make a mess at Francie's front door, if you get my meaning."

"So you went with these girls, met their brother and fell in love, and decided you want to work on the dude ranch instead, so you can plan a future with him."

Hannah looked distraught. "Just be quiet, Taylor. You don't know what it's like to meet the man of your dreams and have him look right through you."

It was news to me that Hannah had ever dreamed

about a cowboy, or rancher, or whatever this guy was. But it was clear that she wasn't inventing her reaction to Jacob.

This wasn't the moment to remind her that we were both supposed to be on our way out of Serendipity forever. She needed to get this guy out of her system, and I knew there was nothing I could say to make a difference.

So I would be supportive. "Maybe next time you see him, he won't be so distracted. I bet he's just focused on getting everything ready so they can open and start making money."

She brightened. "You think so?"

"Seems likely, I'd say. When will that be?"

"First of June. They've got some bookings already, yet the bunkhouse isn't even done."

"Now, see? That's gotta be stressful. You keep learning about horses, and when Jacob's business is running smoothly and he opens his eyes, there you'll be, all knowledgeable and looking awesome in skin tight jeans, boots, and a—I swallowed, trying not to gag—and a plaid shirt."

Smiling, she floated out the door on that note. I almost laughed out loud at the vision of Hannah trying to get on a horse. She wasn't comfortable around big dogs, for Heaven's sake. I couldn't imagine her getting close enough to a horse to even pet it. I had no doubt that she would get Jacob's attention, but she was going to be in for a hard fall when they decided to call it quits, so she could get on with her life.

Good thing I was keeping my eyes on our future, instead of getting sidetracked by a handsome man who was completely wrong for me.

CHAPTER SEVEN

KEN AND I had developed a routine. He always had me doing grunt stuff like constantly cleaning glassware and polishing what felt like acres of furniture, until I could see my reflection in it.

Some of the furniture he called *primitive*. All I had to do to those pieces was dust. Even that seemed pointless to me, because of the worn-off or chipped paint. Some of the wood had never been painted at all, but was wearing its natural *patina*, he called it. That primitive furniture looked like it ought to be in a landfill. I was amazed the first time I sold a primitive chair. After the customers left, I said, "For that price they could have bought a new one."

Ken shook his head, like he was disappointed. "Antique furniture is built to last. Can you imagine a chair bought new today lasting a hundred years, like the one we just sold?"

"Well, maybe not. But who wants to look at the same chair for a hundred years?"

He grinned.

"You know what I mean. Buy the dumb chair and have it the rest of your life—why? It's more fun to buy a new one."

The grin disappeared. "Taylor, you have a lot to learn."

That was bull. I had graduated college and was on my way to an interesting life. I just needed to get over the speedbump of getting a real job.

"Well, Ken, I'm here polishing old stuff all day long. If I'm not learning, it's because you're not teaching me.

He looked into my eyes. It was unsettling, like he was deciding something important about me.

Then he nodded, shifted his stance. "All right. Tomorrow your education begins in earnest."

I should have kept my mouth shut. My job went from drudgery to drudgery with frequent lectures and occasional pop quizzes. But some of the information about antiques sank in, and was actually interesting. Who knew?

The problem was, when Ken spoke passionately on a topic, the very air in the room became energized. The items surrounding us went from inventory to markers of history. I had to be careful not to fall under his spell.

****

I had been working at Once Upon a Time for a few weeks when a couple of burly guys carried in an entire Victorian living room suite, complete with fringe-shaded lamps for the side tables.

Ken had shown them the space we cleared in preparation for this delivery. At first I thought he owned everything in the store, but about half of it was consignment. He'd explained this arrangement soon after I started working there. "Consignors pay a monthly fee for the space, and fix it up the way they want. Subject to my approval of course. We keep their sales receipts calculated separately from mine, and we get to keep a percentage."

"Who's this *we* you keep talking about?"

"You work here, so I'm including you as a person who performs tasks."

Hmm. That sounded logical on its face, but for no reason at all, it made me wonder about Ken's *We* history. In spite of myself, I wondered about it more each day. His *We History*, and his current *We Status*. Was there a girlfriend hidden away somewhere? I didn't want him to know where my mind occasionally wandered, though. I flashed a smile.

"So—*we* get a commission off every consignment sale."

He sighed. "All right, *I* get a commission, and you get a guaranteed hourly wage, whether or not anything sells. Are you saying you prefer commission?"

I did some quick mental math and knew that would be a huge mistake. "No, thanks. I'm good."

Ken and I tweaked the new set-up for way longer than made sense to me, and the Victorian room looked awesome, considering what there was to work with. I didn't like the furniture. The wood was dark, the carvings were so ornate they reminded me of gargoyles. It was just too fussy looking, and the lampshades and lace doilies made it even worse.

"Do you think this will sell?" I asked. "Ever?"

He stood, still appraising the *room*. "Yes, eventually, though Victorian isn't in heavy demand. It will require a special buyer."

"No accounting for taste."

"We're not here to tell people what they like, but to give them options."

Later that day, the same guys came in, carrying a trunk. "Sorry," one of them said. "We didn't realize this trunk was supposed to go with that other stuff. You wouldn't believe the house we're clearing out."

Ken frowned. I knew he was ticked because we'd already spent so much time making that *room* look perfect to him. He had the guys set the trunk in the walkway, and after they were gone he started re-arranging. I tried the latch and was surprised that the lid of the trunk opened easily.

"What did you expect to see in there?" Ken's voice was soft, and nearer than I realized. I looked up and was surprised he seemed interested in my answer.

I closed it, and stood, wiping my hands on the seat of my pants. "I'm glad it's empty. What a shame if someone's personal treasures ended up on display for everyone to see. And to buy." That just seemed wrong.

He stopped fussing with furniture, cocked his head, and gave me his full attention. "I'm guessing lots of the things in this store were once somebody's treasures. Don't you think?"

My mind was on another trunk and its contents. They'd been Opal's treasures, and now they were my treasures. I would never sell them, or put them somewhere that people could paw through them. I would never let any of the things from my trunk end up on the wall of a down home restaurant, as *country decor*. I could imagine one of Opal's diaries, splayed open, maybe with her locket necklace and a lace-trimmed handkerchief, ending up in a shadow box over a table with a fake kerosene lamp made in China. I shivered at the thought.

Ken was looking at me funny. "Now what's wrong? You shivered. Are you getting sick?"

"Sick of people. Of the lack of respect for personal property. And I'm really tired of staring at this gargoyle furniture. Can I take my lunch hour now?" I needed to get out.

"You already had your lunch hour, remember?" He leaned down, looked into my eyes. "We've accomplished a lot, Taylor. Why don't you go out and take a walk. Clear your head. I'll see you back in a little while."

It was one of the kindest things he'd said to me. Just what I needed, and totally unexpected. I was in a rush to get out of there, away from all the furniture, dishes, and decor items that suddenly embodied hundreds of broken dreams. So great was my hurry that I hit the door without grabbing my purse. So, no phone. And no money to stop at the soda fountain. The lack of funds was the bigger problem, since everyone I would want to text was busy at work, or busy having a better life than me.

But the fresh air helped. Instead of dropping in on Mom, or taking a stroll around the perimeter of the square, I steamed up Market Street, heading west. Before I knew it, I was passing Aunt Jacquie's house, and then Gran's.

I missed Gran, and was eager for her to get back from her trip to Canada to stay with friends. I passed her house and continued down to the sidewalk by the highway, across the footbridge and up by the library.

On a whim I stopped in, talked to the desk clerk. When I got back to the shop, I was lugging a couple of tomes about antiques, and a romance novel. No library card—it was in a drawer at home, and it turns out, needed to be updated. But the clerk knew me. Once I told her which twin I was, we took care of the update and I checked out the books.

When I went back into Once Upon a Time, the bell jingled and Ken appeared, looking concerned. "Hey. Feeling better?"

"Yeah, I guess." I shifted the books, which were heavy. "I mean, yes, I am feeling better. Thanks for suggesting the walk. It helped. I stopped by the library while I was out." I was embarrassed for him to see what I had chosen. Should have put them in Mom's van. I set the books under the counter, spines hidden, and arranged my big handbag on top. It was none of his business what I read in my free time, after all.

And it was none of his business if I had realized part

of me *did* care about my job a little more each day. I was sure he'd be surprised to learn that, but no more surprised than I.

After that, work was transformed, because my perception of it changed so much. I didn't mind the hours, the customers who browsed without purchasing, the never-ending cleaning made necessary because dust and grit floated in from the busy square each time the door opened. But so did potential customers. Just not nearly often enough.

In the evenings, after Hannah and I had cleared the table and washed and put away dishes, we sometimes went to our separate rooms instead of hanging out together. I knew she was learning about dude ranches, horses—heck, maybe even the right way to build a bonfire suitable for hot dogs and marshmallows.

Meanwhile, I immersed myself in the world of antiques. The topic was overwhelming, since it could include anything twenty-five years or more old. The biggest library book had photos of furniture and bibelots—which I learned meant a small object of curiosity, beauty, or rarity—back to the Middle Ages. One room pictured in the book reminded me of a long-ago school trip to the Speed Museum in Louisville. I could still almost picture the heavily carved, paneled walls and furniture that was so ornate it looked like it could come alive. And as if some of King Arthur's knights might have sat in the chairs.

Of course, our shop didn't have anything that old, unless Ken had it hidden away in his third floor apartment. What did that look like, anyway? Was he a closet Ikea guy? That would be hysterical.

There were some trunks pictured in the books, but nothing quite like mine. For my own enjoyment, I created an imaginary history for Opal's trunk—it had been made in Boston, hinges created by Paul Revere. That sounded good. And when Opal's ancestors headed out west to homestead, the trunk was packed with the family Bible and other items they couldn't bear to leave behind. A couple of generations later, it became storage for homemade quilt tops until the quilting group could get together to add the batting, the back, and sit around gossiping and quilting with those insanely tiny stitches quilters can do.

What I knew from the diaries what that when Opal was thirteen, she was given the trunk by her grandmother, to use as a hope chest. She put her diaries in it, and over time, added more while her hopes grew, she fell in love, and her wedding to Jeremiah was planned.

I knew about the wedding, every detail of it, because I had read all the diaries. I had read the last one more times than any of the others. How I wished I knew the end—or, maybe I didn't really want to know.

The wedding gown looked perfect, as if it had never been worn. Reading the final diary entry always made me cry. What would it be like to love a man so deeply, to plan the event that united them as man and wife, and never see it happen?

Back when we discovered the trunk, Hannah also seemed enthralled by it. But her interest waned over time.

Even when I insisted that Hannah listen to, or read, the last few diaries and especially the final one, she wasn't as affected as I was. Not even close.

"Can't you just see all the plans she made?" I asked.

"See them? No. I could try to imagine, I guess..." But she wasn't inclined to try.

I had enough enthusiasm for both of us. "Oh, I know just what it looked like. The way they moved all the furniture on the first floor to make the traffic flow better for a houseful, in case of rain. How Opal's brothers pushed the piano to the window so the music could be heard if they did get to have the wedding outside. The chairs and tables, the flowers and all the rest—Well, she describes it so clearly, it's just like you're there when you read it."

Hannah shook her head. "*You*, not me. I'm sorry,

Taylor. It's interesting and all, but I'm just not caught up in it like you are. Maybe show it to one of the girls and you'll get a better reaction."

"No way. This is our secret. We don't have any friends who could appreciate it the way we—"

She held up a hand. "The way *you* do. Yeah, you're probably right. Even Mom wasn't that into it, and she's real sentimental. At least you know I'm not going to fight you for that trunk when we leave home."

Mom and Dad had been interested in the trunk and its contents when we asked permission to bring it to our room. Ben was old enough to help Dad carry it carefully down the steep attic stairs. When it was in the space we had created for it, I put the diaries and wedding trousseau back inside, and closed the lid.

When we got separate rooms, a few months before high school graduation, the trunk went with me because Hannah said I was obsessed with it. I chose an out-of-the-way corner for it, and never piled things on it beyond some favorite stuffed animals. I figured Opal wouldn't mind, and might even be glad to be surrounded by the happy and colorful collection.

Even though I knew the trunk was old, its value as an antique had never occurred to me. I was thankful now that our parents hadn't seen the thing as extra cash. From what I read in the library book, and in online research, the trunk might bring a few hundred dollars if the right buyer could be found. And the wedding dress—so pristine with the filmy veil, and sweet little white leather shoes. Some people collected vintage clothes. Some sold them online. But neither of those possibilities would happen to Opal's things, if I had anything to say about it. No matter how much I'd love to have some extra money, selling the trunk or its contents wasn't an option.

One night, I dreamed that Ken Abernathy bought the trunk from Dad, and hid it away in his third floor apartment behind the locked door, where I could never see it again. The diaries, the dress, all lost to me forever. I woke up sobbing and couldn't get to sleep again.

At the store that day, I kept distance between myself and my boss, suddenly wary of his motivations. To take someone's most prized possession, like he had done in my dream, was heartless. I told myself not to blame *Awake Ken* for what *Dream Ken* had done, but couldn't quite shake the feelings from the nightmare.

When I got back from lunch that day, he was finishing with a customer who bought a set of 1950s drinking glasses. The woman chattered about childhood memories of a set of these polka-dotted glasses. "I broke the orange one," she said. "I think I was more upset about it than Mom was. At some point she got rid of the remaining ones before she died." Sadness washed over the woman's face before she brightened again. "And now I have a complete set. I wonder if my brother will remember them. I'll send him a photo tonight."

She left with her package, and I went behind the counter to stow my handbag. Ken finally stepped aside, leaving me barely enough space to do that.

I grabbed the polishing rag, and turned to go to the back of the store where I'd left off.

"You feeling better after lunch?" Ken asked my retreating back.

"I'm fine." I started cleaning glassware, holding each piece up to the light to be sure it sparkled from every angle. In my peripheral vision I saw Ken approach, but ignored him.

He was two feet away when he cleared his throat. "What's wrong, Taylor? You've been in a mood all day."

I turned on him. "A mood, huh? I've just been here doing my job, Mr. A. Nothing unusual."

"Please just tell me why you're mad at me."

"Mad? At you?"

"Believe me, I know how it looks when a woman is angry with me. In this case, I don't have a clue of the cause, though."

Why did my ridiculous heart skip a beat to hear him refer to me as a woman? I'd gone from being an employee to having an acknowledged gender. This was *not* important to me. And it made my dream-founded irritation with him morph into something else. He was back to being a version of the freaky weird vampire because of taking, and then hiding, the trunk from me. Now in real life, the way he looked at me felt dangerous and sexy.

I wondered if I should have skipped the energy drink and had actual food for lunch.

I was silent for a while, did some more polishing, before making eye contact. I hoped I had myself under control. When I set down the cloth and faced him, I got that flash I'd had the first time we met.

I know you, my brain was saying.

He chuckled. "Good to hear, since I've been writing your paychecks for a few weeks now."

I clapped a hand over my mouth. I had said it out loud.

"I—um——Ken, have you ever thought about the stories these antiques have?" He would say no, and think I was weird.

He frowned in concentration. "You mean like the woman who bought the drinking glasses?"

I shook my head. "Well, that is kind of fun. Sort of a happy ending for her, I guess. But what I mean is, do you think about how each item has a history? A family that loved it, packed it into a box when they moved to a bigger house, set it out with pride when they settled in? Like the cradle that's upstairs—how many babies slept in it? Did the cradle get handed from one generation to the next in a family, until a twenty-first century mom decided it wasn't safe for her baby, and put it into a sale?" I stopped, short of breath from my long speech. "Things like that. Do you?"

His eyes were wide. Shocked? Freaked out?

"I sometimes think about the stories. No doubt each piece here has a history I'd be interested in hearing. My respect for history is part of why I'm here."

"If you—well, do you have an antique that's so special you would never sell it, no matter how much money was offered?"

He considered. "I have a few family pieces that are very dear to me. I wouldn't want to part with those. Each time I look at them, I think of the original owners."

I nodded, liking and trusting him more.

"Do you have something like that, Taylor? Is that why you brought this up?"

I didn't want to go into specifics, but since I'd started the conversation, I had to answer. "I have some old things that are special to me. But they aren't from our family. They were in the house when my parents bought it. I've sort of claimed them."

He waited, then decided I wasn't going to share more. "Sounds very special," he said. "See? I knew there was a reason I hired you. It isn't often an employee feels a real affinity for the work. That's ideal. We're both lucky, aren't we, Taylor?"

I nodded mutely. He went upstairs to rearrange a space after an earlier sale had left a hole. I polished, and sparkled, and let myself think about Ken as a man, and not just my boss.

What guy did I know who could have gotten through that conversation without cracking up laughing?

Good old Ken wasn't like other guys I knew. That felt like a plus, but I wondered if it might also become a problem down the line.

CHAPTER EIGHT

ONE MORNING, MOM didn't take the time to prepare anything for dinner. In her van on the way to town, since there was nothing interesting to talk about, I asked why.

"So, Mom, are you and Dad having a date night? I noticed you didn't set up the slow cooker or anything. I mean, no problem. Hannah and I can grab something." There were enough fast food joints in Serendipity to eat at a different one every day, and that's without including carry-out pizza places.

"Tonight is the city council meeting, Taylor. You've heard us talking about it, right?"

Maybe I had drifted out of the conversation when they talked about boring stuff like that. "Are you on the city council? But—we don't live in the city."

She sighed and shook her head. "Tonight the council is going to discuss the possibility of attracting a big box chain store to town. A massive square footage combination of grocery, retail, pharmacy, and auto service. The possibility of a hypermarket was brought up at a previous meeting. A lot of the local business owners are opposed to it."

"Hypermarket? That sounds energetic."

She wasn't amused. "Without using a particular brand of store, it means a large footprint discount retailer that contains a combination of the elements I mentioned, and possibly more. Think how apt the term is."

I stored *hypermarket* in my brain for future use. "Of course the local business owners are against the idea. Nobody in Serendipity ever wants progress. Would a store like even consider locating here? I don't see how they could make money, considering the size of our population. I mean, even when you consider the whole county."

"I don't know how much of a possibility there is, but you know how rumors and gossip blow things out of proportion. The matter is on the council's agenda, and we want to be there to hear, in person, what is said. Maybe it's nothing. But either way, we need make sure the city government knows how we feel." She glanced at me. "I take it you're not interested. You can text Hannah and have her come to town and pick you up, or wait for me at the shop until the meeting's over. It could be long. I don't know."

I didn't get further into it with her. Poor Mom and Dad, wanting Serendipity to stay the way it had always been. But since it had always been a dead-end place, I didn't understand their point of view.

Unfortunately I wasn't going to get out of thinking about the whole drama, because Ken announced that he was going to the meeting too. "Starts at six," he said, so we need to be sure and close on time."

As if I wasn't always ready to hear the lock click behind me as close to five-thirty as possible.

"I probably shouldn't ask, but where do you stand on the hypermarket thing, Ken?"

His expression was incredulous. "Against it, of course. What did you expect?"

I fiddled with a display of ornate letter openers. "Oh, I don't know. Since you've lived somewhere else, I thought maybe you were open-minded about change."

His brows furrowed. "Change can be a great thing for a town, but not this kind of change. Do you know what will happen if a big box store like that locates in Serendipity?"

I held up a hand and started counting on my fingers. "Let's see, there will be more jobs."

He nodded. "Minimum wage jobs, and except for a handful of managers, most would be only part-time. Not a job that could sustain a household, even if two adults worked there. Your next point?"

Hmm. "Well, more shopping for us. I mean, there's a lot of stuff you can't buy without driving to the Louisville area."

"If a big box discounter is your kind of shopping destination, there are two you can get to in half an hour, and four others in an hour."

"That's ridiculous. To drive half an hour to buy—I don't know—paper towels."

"Our local groceries sell paper towels. So do the dollar stores."

"Okay, that was a bad example. How about clothes?"

"The type of clothes you can get at someplace like that is available at dollar stores we already have. You don't shop at a grocery slash retailer for clothes, I'm guessing."

I considered it a compliment that he realized that. "Of course not. But a lot of people do. I bet most people in our county would love to have a massive place under one roof where they could buy produce, clothes, shampoo, and a set of tires."

He stared out the big plate glass window at the town square. "Think of it another way, Taylor. How many locally-owned shops would be driven out of business by something like that?"

"Well, not this one. You can't buy antiques in a place like that." Not that many people were buying antiques at Once Upon a Time.

"Right. But what do you think will happen to the jewelry store, the hardware store, the locally-owned pharmacies, and the groceries? Even the Bible bookstore would probably be in trouble. Think about all the businesses in town that are long-established, contribute to all kinds of community events, and support the schools in various ways. I can name a dozen that won't last six months if a hypermarket is built here."

So he wasn't worried about his own store. "What if it brought new people to Serendipity, to shop? That could be business for us, right? And for the locally-owned restaurants, and some other shops?"

He shook his head. "A place like that would be built far enough from the square that anyone driving to town for it would be likely to stay right around there. They'd probably have a gas station—there's another group of endangered businesses eventually standing empty. And fast food shops would pop up around it. Possibly fast food places downtown would relocate. I've seen it happen."

For someone relatively young, his attitude was sure conservative. "Thanks for your insight, Ken. I get that you're down on big box stores, and sure, it's nice to have little mom and pop businesses, but that's not the real world."

"I'm not talking real world, Taylor. I'm talking Serendipity. This town has a chance to capitalize on its uniqueness, bring people in for a relaxing stay. Francie's B&B and the new dude ranch are just a couple of examples. The guests who stay there won't be impressed by a hypermarket. They can shop in one of those anywhere. They'll be drawn to unique places, and to our beautiful downtown—unless we let it die. Unless we actively work toward shutting it down by bringing a big box store in. I've seen it happen, as I said before. Nice town, had some issues, but had some things going for it, too. Instead of working together to create a strategic plan to build on the town's assets, it's easy to look for salvation from outside. What is the point of trying to create a miniature replica of the metro area?"

"You talk about strategic planning. What else is there to bring tourists here?"

"The beautiful courthouse. Give tours of it on

weekends. Have the chamber of commerce open on the weekends, so folks can get information about sights to see while they're here. We've got a flyer promoting local business, and all of the Square Merchants have those flyers available, which is a small step. That's actually very recent. Until the last year or so, there was nothing for people to hold in their hand that told them about the restored grist mill, or how close we are to two state parks. And hiking, camping, and fishing at the county-owned park. "

His enthusiasm was starting to get to me. "Is there a website? A Facebook page?"

"Yes, and those things are recent, too, but they're great tools. I talked to some of the local tech teachers about creating a Serendipity app, but so far it isn't viable yet."

An app about our town? That would be amazing. "There's so much you could do with an app."

"I know. Like I said, we're trying to think big, and even if some things fall through, it's better to fail than never try. A big box is an investment in failure. Even local law enforcement doesn't like the idea. They've researched neighboring towns' experiences, and were alarmed at the increase in crime, additional police officers needed, more strain on the court system from the thefts and scams. Evidently there are people who actually work a circuit of that type of store. If the thing comes in, they'll want a huge tax abatement, which means it won't be paying for the extra pressure on the city and county."

Deflated, I sank into a Louis IV chair.

"So how are we going to keep all this from happening?"

CHAPTER NINE

ON MY LUNCH hour, sitting in the little back corner eating my ham and cheese sandwich and apple, I texted Hannah. It showed how concerned Mom was about the meeting that she hadn't let Hannah know she'd need to find something for dinner on her own. Since it was a week night, she might eat dinner with Emily, or just go home and raid the fridge, which had some fine leftovers.

I was glad Hannah's lunch hour and mine didn't coincide. I didn't want to talk to her on the phone about how important this meeting might be. I knew she wouldn't understand the complications of a possible hypermarket any more than I had. Like me, she wouldn't even be familiar with the term that I'd heard way too many times today.

We had more people than usual in the store that afternoon, and most of them weren't looking for antiques. They wanted to talk to Ken about the meeting. He listened to those who differed with him, and offered some facts and figures to support his stand. At almost closing time the store was finally empty, except for us.

"You joining us at Chez Gwen for dinner?" he asked.

"There's time for that before a meeting that starts at six?"

"Gwen's setting up a special buffet in the basement dining room. When we knew the meeting date for sure, the merchant group worked it out. If the discussion goes long, there could be lots of growling stomachs." He grinned, and I pulled a face.

"Nice. Thanks for that reminder. Well, I guess I could swing dinner." Chez Gwen was known for delicious, and for our town, upscale food. But cheap it was not. Since Dad had scuttled the gravy train, and my money was hard-earned, I had learned to be more cautious than ever with it. In my eagerness to get out of town and start my life, leftovers and cold sandwiches were more appealing than in the past. So far Mom and Dad hadn't charged us to live with them, but Dad had made noises about us pitching in for groceries. I had to admit that was more than fair.

Ken watched me. Maybe I was obviously weighing my options, which, with half an hour, and no car at my disposal, were pretty slim. "How about I buy your dinner?" he asked. "Your attendance at the meeting will help represent Once Upon a Time, after all."

"Wow. Really? That makes me feel all official." I kind of hoped I agreed with whatever Ken said at the meeting. Otherwise, the situation at work could get awkward. I sure couldn't afford to lose my job. "Thanks for buying dinner. But...it won't look like we're on a date, right?"

He frowned, and I thought he was going to say something rotten. Then he reached into a pocket and peeled a bill out of a money clip. "Here. Buy your dinner with no chance of gossip. You're right, people around here will certainly talk about anything. I'm still learning that."

"Well. Thanks." It occurred to me that rumors about me dating Ken would be kind of enjoyable. He was attractive and smart, interested in the community. Very different from anyone I'd dated in high school or college. "I'll keep track of the change, and give it to you tomorrow."

He opened the door and I grabbed my bag from under the counter. "Good enough. Shall we?"

Mom was coming up the sidewalk, which made Ken and me obviously not a couple to everyone driving around the square.

"Your daughter is coming with us this evening, Jennifer."

Mom slid an arm through mine. "Oh, my. I'm so glad. I guess you've been filling her with propaganda today?"

I looked from her to Ken. Would he be offended?

But he laughed. "Absolutely. Once Upon a Time seemed to be anti-hypermarket central today. Folks were in and out constantly, just to talk. Our grand total of sales was five dollars and tax."

Mom cringed. "Ouch. But it was the same at my shop. Not just business owners, but lots of concerned citizens. I'd say about half of my visitors were in favor of the new store, though. I tried to help explain the drawbacks. Maybe they'll show up at the meeting and be part of the discussion. Wouldn't it be wonderful if we had so many people interested, the meeting had to move somewhere larger because the council chambers couldn't hold everyone?"

"It's good for folks to be interested in government matters," Ken said. We were at the door of Chez Gwen, which was only about a block from Ken's store. Carla Standish was locking her dress shop next door. Ken opened and held the restaurant door while Mrs. Glass, Carla, Mom and I walked in.

Aunt Darlene, looking very chic and powerful, was in the waiting area with Dad and Uncle Jamison. Dad gave Mom a quick kiss on the cheek. Then he looked at me, obviously surprised.

I stood up straighter. "I'm here to help Ken, in case he doesn't remember he's against a big box retailer, instead of for it." Everybody chuckled, and Uncle Jamison told the hostess we were with the group eating in the basement, and could find our way there. She smiled and waved us on.

I hadn't been in the Chez Gwen basement for several years. Two walls were plain brick, and the other two painted a pretty silvery grey. There were surprisingly good paintings by local artists, nice carpet, tables with white linen cloths, and potted silk ferns that looked real. There was a bar too, but that was left over from a previous owner. The strongest drink you can get at Chez Gwen these days is their awesome sweet tea. I ordered a glass, thinking the sugar and caffeine might be a good idea.

The buffet was roast beef, fried chicken, mashed potatoes, gravy, sweet potatoes, two kinds of salads, homemade yeast rolls that I remembered were to-die-for. Dessert was extra, but I didn't need it after that spread. In spite of the caffeine, I wasn't real energetic. Instead, my very full tummy made me feel taking a nap.

I also wasn't a bit sure about spending more time with Ken. Somehow I'd ended up seated between him and Uncle Jamison. They'd had plenty to talk about, and I felt as if I was in the way, yet more and more in sync with what was being said. Why, again, had I thought Serendipity needed a hypermarket?

CHAPTER TEN

THE CROWD BARELY fit into the city council's meeting room, with some of us spending the entire time standing up, leaning against a wall. I didn't mind, though. It wasn't like I wanted to go up and make a speech.

The meeting lasted three hours. Lots of people did want to make speeches. Fortunately the folks in favor of the big box store were less organized than those of us who were against it. The council listened to everybody though. I had to give them credit for seeming very open-minded. It looked like they wanted to do the will of the people, which is what I'd thought democracy was about. But you never know.

Aunt Darlene was the last to speak. Her remarks were eloquent, well thought-out, and unemotional, just what I'd expect of her. After a few minutes, the council voted to table the idea of seeking a big box store to come to Serendipity.

The anti-big-box contingent cheered. I don't know when I'd been so relieved.

Then the council president banged his gavel. "Folks, this matter is set aside for now. But you all know we need more employment in our city and county." He gestured at Jared Barnett. "Jared is doing a good job of bringing new businesses in, but so far they're small, and it will take a while to see sizable benefit to the community."

Jared nodded slightly at the mention of his name. Carla was standing next to him, and looked ready to jump down the throat of anyone who said her husband wasn't doing a good job. But surely everyone realized Serendipity hadn't gotten in such a mess with employment overnight, and it couldn't be fixed overnight either. I mean, even I understood that, and I hadn't paid all that much attention. Factory jobs went overseas, and the factories shut down and sat empty. We only had working factories left, including the one Uncle Jamison and my dad ran.

Years ago at the company picnic, Hannah and I had noticed big family groups there. "Some of the people who work for us are third generation," Dad had explained.

Where would you find three-generation employment these days?

The woman next to me yawned loudly enough that I

started to yawn, too. Then I came back to what the council president was saying.

"I'm asking all of you to help Jared, your city council, and the county government. We all want what's best for our community, and maybe one of you, or a group of you, will come up with ideas we're not thinking of. So when you leave here tonight, instead of concentrating on the specifics of tonight's discussion, please put your minds to work on creative ideas to help our community." He looked at the other city council members, who nodded soberly, then picked up his gavel. "We meet the same time each month. We're here to serve you. Anything that needs to be on the agenda, please call the mayor's office a week ahead of time." He rapped the gavel on the wooden desk.

I thought there might be another big cheer, or some sign of celebration, but everyone talked quietly on their way out. No war was won tonight. Just a battle, and we didn't know when the next might occur. Serendipity's strategic planning committee needed to get in gear.

Except, as far as I knew, there wasn't one.

CHAPTER ELEVEN

IT WAS NICE to get out of the store in the middle of the workday, so when the weather was pleasant, I sometimes went to the park to eat my sandwich. Sometimes when there was rain, I sat in Mom's van instead of hanging out in the back room at Once Upon a Time, or feeling like I should do laundry at Emily's Dreams.

Today's invitation from my Aunt Jacquie was way better than any of those. I couldn't imagine how she made much money with her quirky little coffee house just off the square. But I'm also not sure making money was the point. It's almost like Aunt Jacquie was just there to talk to whoever needed to vent. Plus the coffee and homemade scones were outstanding.

Just a block away, at Something Sweet, you could order a cake, buy cookies, brownies, and doughnuts of all sorts. Aunt Jacquie wasn't competing with them, she was just...sort of hanging out. And—scones? In small town Indiana? It was typical of her to serve the unusual.

The whole time we were growing up, my mother's sister Jacqueline was this shadowy figure nobody talked about much. She went all over the country as a travel writer, and we spent our annual family vacation with her, wherever she was living at the time.

There wasn't a negative feeling about Aunt Jacquie, just a hole in our family for the rest of the year, I guess. Mom was real close friends with her now that she had moved back to Serendipity, and any time I saw my aunt and grandmother together, I was struck by how much they loved spending time with each other. They must have missed each other like crazy while Aunt Jacquie was gone.

Maybe that's how Mom would feel, once Hannah and I were gone for good.

Just to clarify, both of my aunts are unique. Aunt Darlene is a beautiful, successful businesswoman, who participates in some of the local community betterment projects. But Aunt Darlene has never quite figured out how to be pleasant to people. When we were growing up, her aloofness seemed to put her in the category of Someone Important. But we eventually learned it's more that she's Someone Difficult.

Then there's Aunt Jacquie, without a doubt Someone Special.

Aunt Jacquie always understood people so well, and knew what they needed before they did. She was the best listener in the world. She never interrupted, and listened with her whole self, to everything you said. Your mannerisms, even—nothing escaped her. It might have been eerie if Aunt Jacquie wasn't one of the kindest people I'd ever met.

Emily was more like Aunt Jacquie than Hannah or I. All that weirdness that happened when Emily was running the Emily's Dreams shop—selling her own stuff, almost everything she owned. That was odd enough, even though on the face of it, she was trying to make whatever income she could, in spite of being on a cane and unable to work a regular job. The really odd thing was when Emily *gave* things away, often something small, maybe seemingly insignificant. Sometimes that item turned out later to be life-changing for the person she gave it to.

We were lucky to have Jacquie as our aunt, and everyone in Serendipity was lucky she came back to town after being gone for years.

Especially, of course, Nick Marshall. You could see the love burning in his eyes whenever Aunt Jacquie was in sight. They were a beautiful couple, perfectly matched, and I could see them being married for fifty years, like I could see my parents that way.

I was glad for them, but I wasn't looking for a relationship like that. I didn't want to be tied down the way they were, unable to make a unilateral decision. That wasn't the life for me. When Hannah woke up from her cowboy dream, she'd remember she didn't want that kind of life either.

So today's hour with Aunt Jacquie was a treat. I had my sack lunch from home and she put a carafe of aromatic coffee, two thick white mugs, and a plate of scones in the center of the small table. Then she sat across from me and opened her own lunch bag.

"Tell me about yourself, Taylor," she invited. "We need to catch up."

I don't know why she's so easy to talk to, but I found myself unloading all my hopes and dreams on her, and somehow along the way I must have said something about Ken, and the trunk. I'm not sure why that all rushed out.

"So tell me what you've learned from reading that girl's diaries. It sounds like those have had a big impact on you."

"Oh, maybe not such a big impact. I mean, Hannah and I probably would have planned to leave Serendipity without them."

"But—I thought the girl in the diaries lived in Serendipity. That she was happy."

"Well, yes, she was, but you know, the diaries end suddenly, and that can only mean something terrible happened."

"And that something was..."

I shrugged. "I think the guy didn't show up for the wedding. I've heard of jerks like that. Maybe he had another girlfriend the whole time, and this girl—Opal—she was oblivious of it because she was blindly in love with him. It's so tragic."

"So you've decided not to be a tragic figure like her."

"Well, yes. Of course."

"And you think that in order to avoid tragedy, you'll keep love at arm's length?"

I nodded, wondering where she was going with this.

"What if you happen to fall in love in spite of your good intentions?"

Now, this I could deal with. "I'm not going to let that happen. I'll date, have a good time, but if any guy wants to get serious, I'll tell him good-bye. I've seen what that girl built herself up to, what her dreams were, and then her fiancée broke her heart."

"But, Taylor, you don't really know what happened, do you?"

"Well, no. But it couldn't be anything else. If the wedding had taken place, she would have written about it in her diary. If she had called it off, she would have felt empowered, and would have recorded that." I sighed. "Nope. It can only be a matter of him breaking her heart. When I re-read that last diary, with the details of the wedding right down to the flowers in the buttonholes, I know she was committed. I feel like I know her after reading years' worth of diaries. She didn't want that much out of life—just a good marriage and children. You know, normal stuff for women in that time period. And yet she didn't get it. I know she didn't."

Aunt Jacquie pushed the plate of scones toward me. "And that means you can never have a marriage and children?"

I shook my head at both the question and the extra scone. "I learned from her example. Falling so desperately in love is a dead end. She didn't have anything else planned for her life except to be Jeremiah's wife. Nope, that would never be my path. Because of her I've always known I wanted a career far away from here, with no man holding me back from my potential."

She leaned back in her chair. "Oh, Taylor. Potential can be achieved whether or not there's a man in your life. I had a successful career before coming back to Serendipity to help Mother after her fall, and a completely different type of success now I'm here, and married to Nick. I worry about you and Hannah reading too much into the diaries of a woman you never knew."

But I did know Opal. "Hannah's not into the contents of the trunk like I am. And, I don't know, she seems to be interested in some local guy right now. I'm sure it's temporary, but he's got her attention."

One delicate brow rose. "And you're not interested in any local guy, Taylor?"

My face got hot. Must have had too much coffee. "No—not me. I don't get out to meet anybody interesting."

"Hmm. Ken's interesting, I think."

"You can have him."

She smiled. "No, thanks. I've caught my limit with Nick."

I tried to relax, but couldn't manage it. "I know. I was kidding."

"You don't find Ken somewhat of an enigma?"

"Uh... I just think of him as my boss, the guy who

99

signs the checks. Strictly business between us."

"Oh, right."

She sure had the wrong idea. "Really, Aunt Jacquie. I mean, he's too old for me, and he's got this dead-end business in a dead-end town. Ken Abernathy is the last man in the world I'd want to get involved with."

"He's not that old."

"Well, he's closer to thirty than he is to twenty. And before you bring it up, I'll admit he's good-looking. But he's settled here, running a business with absolutely no future. On the other hand, I can't wait to leave."

I looked at my phone. "Hey, I'm sorry. Lunch hour's almost gone. I need to get back to work, or I'll be in trouble with that handsome guy I'm not attracted to." I laughed, but it wasn't convincing even to me.

As I crossed the courtyard, taking the shortcut back to work, I told myself that my heart was racing because I was in a hurry. It was nothing to do with Ken, or with the way Aunt Jacquie seemed to look directly into my soul and see something I hadn't realized was there.

CHAPTER TWELVE

WHEN I GOT back to work, Ken's greeting took my mind off the path Aunt Jacquie had sent it.

"Taylor, I need to talk to you about something."

Those words are always the start of bad news. Since it was my boss saying them, and he looked worried, plus business really stunk, I could imagine I was about to learn what it felt like to be fired. So I was super glad that Gran and Lillian Standish came in the store just when he was hemming and hawing.

Ken was instantly in gracious-host mode. That's what he seemed like to me when customers were there. It worked well with the way the store was reminiscent of a great big overstuffed house. "Good afternoon, ladies. What can we help you with?"

They blushed prettily at his attention.

Gran said, "Ken, neither of us needs anything, but

it's always a delight to walk through and see what's—well, new, I suppose."

"How about what's been added?" he suggested with a smile.

"That's it," Lillian agreed, picking up an ancient copy of *Anne of Green Gables*. "We were just talking about our book club. Not sure what we'll do for a meeting space if we decide to change from the library. We tend to run long, with lots of good discussion, and often the custodian needs to set up for another event. I wish we could think of another option, because few of us want to host everyone in our homes." She slid *Anne* back onto the shelf and sighed.

An idea popped into my head. "Some place where you could sit and chat about books for a couple of hours in a lovely corner, and maybe have a cup of tea?"

"Oh, Taylor, you'll have us wishing for the impossible," Gran said. "I've thought of something similar, but Chez Gwen can't promise to always have their back room available for us. And a couple of our members wouldn't be able to do the flight of stairs to their basement."

Ken shifted from one foot to the other, probably wanting to get on with firing me. "Maybe one of the downtown churches?"

Gran shook her head. "We've looked into it, even

used one church meeting room for a while. With utilities to heat or cool the room just for us, they needed to charge, and that became awkward. Plus, dragging refreshments in, trying to be sure we cleaned up afterward..."

I could see it in my mind. "What about a store right on the square with plenty of tables and chairs in a quiet back corner, tea served from beautiful pots, delicate cups and saucers, and cucumber sandwiches, or whatever you have with tea? The place is ready when you arrive and stays open 'til, maybe 5:30-ish?"

Gran's eyes sparkled. "And a delightful young lady serves us, and makes the refreshments from, perhaps, family recipes?" She winked at Lillian, who was smiling and nodding.

Then we all looked at Ken.

"Here? Tea and sandwiches? We're not set up for it."

"But we could be," I said. "We have plenty of tables and chairs, loads of china and silverware. Just need to do some re-arranging. I bet we could make that back room into a bare-bones kitchen."

"Oh my, what a wonderful idea," said Lillian. "And you know, it's exactly the kind of quaint little spot our B&B customers are looking for. I get lots of compliments during tree season when I serve their breakfast on good china in my dining room because the Christmas shop isn't available. And with the tea room in the back of the store, everyone would be treated to a walk-through of your showroom, Ken."

He looked at me suspiciously. "You're offering to take this on? Prepare the food, the tea, whatever? And clean it up?"

Since I needed a job for now, my answer was easy. "Sure thing. I think it could be awesome."

When my real job came through, I could train a replacement. How hard could it be?

A customer came in needing Ken's attention, but the ladies and I discussed the tea room for a long while. I made the executive decision that the book club meeting had dibs on the space from three to five-thirty, one Thursday each month. If the way to a man's heart is through his stomach, maybe the checkbook of the shop's owner could be accessed that way, too.

I didn't ask Ken what he had wanted to discuss. The fact that he let it drop made me certain I had been right. Thank goodness for Gran and Lillian's accidental intervention. Once I had the tea room set up, I had an idea they would do a great job of spreading the word. We'd need some type of flyer, or something to put in the tiny cabins—

and maybe the brochure Mom had shown me could be updated to include the tea room.

Was that something to discuss with Jared Barnett? Would I need to be sure Ken did that, and offer to take care of it if he didn't want to?

I had a rough time falling asleep that night, my brain was so busy with ideas and questions. I tried to ignore the ones that were of a personal nature, taking me back to the discussion with Aunt Jacquie.

CHAPTER THIRTEEN

THE BOOK CLUB loved meeting in the tea room. They complimented the fancy sandwiches I served from recipes out of Mom's *Downton Abbey* cookbook. They sighed with pleasure when their delicate cups were filled from the flower-sprigged pot.

I wasn't sure what to charge, and Ken was no help, still expecting the event to be a loser. Gran suggested a dollar amount, and the ladies paid graciously.

In all my insistence that I wouldn't want to be a waitress, it hadn't occurred to me that serving could be enjoyable.

Before leaving, the ladies asked to reserve the space for the following month.

Lillian put a hand on my arm, and glanced at Ken who was near enough to hear but looked like he was trying not to. "Taylor, we'll be discussing *Paris Time Capsule* next month. Is it possible that you could serve something French to go along with the book?"

One of the other ladies joined us. "That's what's called immersive learning, right?" She laughed. "Taylor, this has been such a delightful time. We appreciate you organizing it for us. I wanted to ask, after you have added our next meeting to your calendar, whether I could schedule a small luncheon. It's for my Serendipity High graduating class. We get together every month, and next time is my turn to choose the spot. We're talking fifteen to twenty folks. Not getting any younger, but we sure do have fun together."

Twenty would be more than the space could hold. I hated to say this to her, because it sounded like another good group. My subconscious was working on a lunch menu, when Ken joined us, extending his hand.

"Ken Abernathy. So nice to have you here today."

She took his hand. "Myra Blandings. My son Hank owns the Barbeque Basement, and has offered to let us meet there since their afternoons are slow. But the stairs are a problem for some of us."

The rest of the ladies swooped over, drawn like moths to the light bulb of Ken's charm.

"I'm a fan of the Basement," he said. "Such an unexpected restaurant in a town of this size. Mrs. Blandings,

I'm afraid the current configuration of our tea room won't accommodate your SHS class. But by next month, we will have changed things up. As you know, you're our first guests. Let's go up to the counter, and I'll take your meeting information and phone number. Would that be satisfactory?"

The women floated out a while later. I didn't want to push my luck with Ken's sudden embrasure of the tea room, so I cleaned up the table, pocketing a generous tip, and managed to wash the china and silver in the meager sink, in the poorly-lit back room. I had everything dried and on a big silver tray, and was preparing to return it to the display. I had used items belonging to Ken, not consignment customers.

When I stepped out into the tea room area, he was standing there, his expression unreadable, arms across his chest. But I wouldn't be intimidated. He might not have liked the books and tea idea at first, but now that it was a success, what did he have to complain about?

I had halted in my tracks on seeing him, but forced a brief smile and shifted my load so he would know I was trying to work, and that he was keeping me from it. "Did you need something, Ken? I was going to put these things back on display."

"You think this side project is going to save your job."

"Well, yes, I'd expect that. So I was right in thinking you were planning to fire me?"

He shook his head. "Cut your hours. I know you need the money, Taylor, and there are times I need help."

"Every day in every way," I muttered.

Ken frowned. "What's that?"

"Oh—nothing. Go on. You *were* going to reduce my hours..."

"Because I'm not making enough net profit. Now, with the tea room idea looking like a *possible* way to bring in potential customers—"

I expected some glowing praise. Waited for it to wash over me.

"I'm going to be out money for an upgrade to the back room, and whatever costs are involved with getting a license or whatever to serve food here."

"It's your building," I said. "Can't you do whatever you want in it? I mean, not host a casino, but surely tea and sandwiches are okay."

He uncrossed his arms, shook his head. "Oh, Taylor, you are so young. I'm going up to city hall now, see what they can tell me." He went out the front door.

So much for glowing praise. It was more like glowering acceptance. But as I put the china and silver spoons back on display, I knew he would eventually come around. The tea room was a great idea. Lillian thought so, and she was really smart about business. She knew what her B&B customers wanted, and they would be part of our target market. Ken would eventually have to admit that I'd done him a huge favor by starting the new project.

With no customers in the store, I picked up a dust cloth and walked into one of the window displays, a mahogany table for two with a wine decanter and glasses. My imagination started working on a plan that was even better than the tea room. I hurried to my purse, pulled out my phone, and sent a text to Ken.

While you're at it, find out about serving wine.

Once Upon a Time was about to become very popular, assuming the proprietor could bend a little.

CHAPTER FOURTEEN

THE LAST WORKDAY of the week, Saturday right after closing, I made arrangements with Hannah to pick me up when I texted. I stayed late to help Ken move displays a little, making sure all the consignment spots still had their promised square footage. This reduced the display area for what he owned. I could see it bothered him to make this change. Luckily, I had my eye on the big picture, even if he didn't know there was one.

"This better work," he said. "I'm counting on your tea room to bring in more customers for antiques, you know. Not just to eat and drink, and never come back."

He was like a little boy who'd been told to put away his toys. "I know you don't like to shrink your display area, Ken. If you give the tea room a reasonable try and it doesn't perform for you, it's obviously not that big a deal to switch the floor plan back to antiques only. Which also isn't working." I took a deep breath and plunged into territory probably better left unexplored. "Why stick with this place, anyway? It's not like Serendipity is a hub of commerce. And I'm not sure you could have chosen a deader line of merchandise, if you'll excuse the pun. Surely your uncle would want you to be a success."

His expression changed in an instant, from wary about the tea room to angry at me for my intrusion.

"Leave my uncle out of this."

"But I can't, can I? You're here because of him—watching a failing business head toward bankruptcy. I didn't know him because *like a lot of people*, then and now, I didn't shop here. I just recognized him and thought, *Oh, there's Mr. Hendrickson, the antiques store guy. He's really old, and he always wears a suit.*"

Ken's anger shifted when he recalled his uncle. A hint of a smile lifted a corner of his kissable mouth.

Whoa—kissable? Where had that come from?

He slid the brocade seat of a walnut dining chair under the table. "He was one of a kind. Such a great man. I'm sorry you didn't know him."

"We didn't run with the same crowd, for sure."

Good thing, I hoped, Ken was thinking about his uncle now, instead of worrying that I was shaking the place up too much. Maybe I had said the right thing for once, because we finished moving everything without more personal discussion. I wished we didn't always have to talk about work. I wanted to get to know the real man, who was hiding so effectively behind the mask of store owner and neighborhood nice guy. My first impression of him being a handsome devil had only been half right. Yet any time I tried to peek at the real Ken, he shut me out.

But I could be persistent when I wanted something. Hannah and I pushed for what we wanted, and a lot of times it worked. Without her at my side I couldn't double-team Ken, though. And what I wanted now—a chance to connect with him on a personal level—was so much more important than anything my twin and I had campaigned for over the years.

Because he and I were both somewhat OCD about appearance, putting final touches on the tea room area took longer than expected. When we finished, the space was as homey and inviting as Lillian Standish's dining room, with unnecessary but lovely added touches, like wall-hung flower vases.

In addition to the big walnut table with leaves that we had used for the book club, we had moved in another expandable table and chairs, and created a table for two from a cherry wood tea cart with drop leaves. When not in use for seating, this could be a serving piece in addition to the ornate buffet. Dishes and cutlery for the tea room were stored in, and on, the buffet, except for the delicate cups inverted in their saucers at each place. To stay with the ambiance, we would use linen napkins and tablecloths. That was one negative, because I had an idea it would involve me hauling them home, and returning next morning with clean ones.

Or did Ken have a washer and dryer in his apartment? I wondered, but mostly not because I cared about his laundry facilities.

I stood just outside the space, assessing. "I think it's almost perfect. A chandelier hanging from the ceiling would be awesome, though."

Ken groaned. "I hope you're kidding."

"No, it *would* be awesome. In case a customer wanted this space for, like, a romantic dinner. A chandelier on a dimming switch could set the mood."

He was standing very near, doing his own visual assessment. "But since it's a tea room, and not a setting for a romantic dinner, that's not a mood we're going for."

The rest of the store lights were off, and had been since closing time. Since it was dark outside now, the tea room had become a cozy, intimate space. I turned off the wall switch that controlled the back corner's hideous overhead fluorescents. We were left in the pale glow of a floor lamp with a hand-painted globe, and weak light from the back room spilling through its doorway.

"If you find a stray chandelier among the store contents, I'll consider it." His voice was soft, and very near.

When I turned toward him, my smart aleck reply died on my lips.

In that moment, the handful of years and different life paths that separated us dissolved into the soft darkness around us.

My breath caught, and all thoughts of the tea room, the store, and anything else realistic, were gone.

There was just Ken and me, the beating of our hearts. The electric charge in the air had nothing to do with a chandelier, and everything to do with the attraction that had been simmering in the background ever since we first met.

I don't know if he reached for me, or if I stepped toward him, but suddenly his arms were around me, gentle, and full of promise. His breath was as erratic as mine, which gave me the courage to rise to my tiptoes and touch my lips to his.

He hesitated, and I was afraid I had misread the signs. But the wait was brief, followed by the sweetest kiss—a delicate touch, long and lazy, driving me insane. It was followed by a nibble on my lower lip. I thought I might explode—my body wanted more, while my brain screamed that I was out of my mind.

Maybe Ken was experiencing a similar internal war, because he raised his head and let out an anguished sigh. His arms loosened and I felt cold. "Taylor, I didn't mean for that to happen."

His soft words deflated me.

Self-conscious now, I dropped my arms to my sides, missing the rightness of Ken's taut muscles under my hands. My lips tingled, and my respiration rate wasn't back to normal yet. So my voice came out wispy. "Are you saying you regret kissing me?"

If so, my ego was going to take that news very hard.

His almost-grin began to appear at a corner of his kissable mouth—I'd thought of it that way once, and now I knew I'd been right.

"If you don't regret it, Taylor, I certainly don't. It's—well, since you're my employee, I don't want you to think I'd been planning that. Don't want you to think I expect more of the same, in exchange for your job. That would be wrong, on so many levels."

I twirled a length of hair, a nervous habit I thought I

had left in the past. "I haven't known you long, but I know you're one of the good guys, Ken."

This discussion had killed my mood like a bucket of cold water.

"I wouldn't want to do anything to ruin things between us," he said. "Should we try to pretend the kiss never happened? Make sure it never happens again? We could blame the moment on enthusiasm about the tea room project, coupled with accidental romantic lighting." One eyebrow rose in a question. "I leave it up to you."

He looked as if my answer meant a lot to him.

I shrugged, hoping to look casual. "How about we both think it over instead of making a judgment right now?"

****

I texted Hannah and she drove into town. I was waiting alone by the front door when she pulled up, the headlights bathing the front entryway in brightness that would kill any mood. No matter though—Ken had begun to tackle the back room to make it a more usable kitchen.

"My sister's here. See you in the morning," I called.

"Okay. 'Night, Taylor."

If anyone had heard our exchange, they wouldn't have a clue of what happened between us a little while ago. I could almost believe it was a dream—my world had changed so drastically, and then returned to normal.

I clicked my seat belt, watched him walk to the front and lock the door. I waved, but couldn't tell whether or not he saw me.

"What's weird with you?" Hannah asked a few minutes later when I had answered all her chatter with silence, or uh-huh and mm-hmm.

I leaned my head against the side window. "Just work. Big day."

"No kidding," she said. "Almost twelve hours, and on a Saturday. Should look good on payday, at least."

But I wasn't thinking about the extra money in my paycheck—money that I suspected Ken couldn't afford at this point. I was re-living that bone-melting kiss, and wondering if it was going to change everything.

CHAPTER FIFTEEN

WE GOT THROUGH the evening's pleasantries with Mom and Dad, and went upstairs. I grabbed Hannah's arm, and jerked her into my room.

I closed the door silently, checking to be sure Mom and Dad were still downstairs. "I need to talk."

"What's up with you?" she asked, alarmed. "You don't say a word to me in the car, and now you practically drag me off my feet. Are you in some kind of trouble? Without me?" She looked hurt at the possibility.

I paced the carpet. "I think I might be in trouble. I kissed Ken tonight."

"You..." She slid into a chair, shaking her head. "I thought he was this odd, older character. Right? That's what you've been saying. I've pictured him looking like Tommy Lee Jones. You kissed Tommy Lee Jones?"

"Ken's not that old. Less than thirty. And he's not so

119

odd once you get to know him."

"You kissed your boss. Wow. Just...wow."

"Don't make a big deal out of it."

She frowned. "I'll have a bruise on my arm tomorrow to show *you're* the one making a big deal out of it. So, is he good-looking? Amusing, in a small town sort of way?"

I dropped onto my bed. "Good-looking, funny, kind. And smart, except he's so caught up in trying to run that store the same way it's been run in the past. You know, that old man, Mr. Hendrickson. He was Ken's uncle."

She was nodding. "You already told me that. He has the uncle's store, it's full of antiques, and business isn't good."

"I have some ideas to change things, bring in more business of a new kind. He's going for the tea room, but sort of dragging his feet, ready for it to fail."

Hannah crossed her legs, fiddled with a framed family picture on a table by the chair. "I don't think it will fail, do you?" she asked. "It seems like a cool idea, especially if the tourists pick up on it. Local people, maybe not so much."

I raised onto my elbows. "Gran's book club was all about it. We've had several requests since then. There's actually a lot more on the calendar now than just *take out trash* on Wednesdays."

She giggled. "It all sounds so lame. So very Serendipity."

I bristled. "It isn't lame. It's sort of awesome. We can make the most of the downtown location, the ambiance, and furniture that was built for hospitality."

Hannah let out a breath that ruffled her hair. "Good grief. Since when are you an antique fan?" She jerked a finger toward the corner of my room, where the stuffed animals smiled from their perch. "Besides the trunk, I mean."

"I'm learning to be a fan. All of the antiques have stories. Being in one of those little display areas is almost like being in a house a long time ago. It's cozy, and you feel kind of loved."

Her eyes narrowed. "Loved by furniture?"

I was getting exasperated, and only part of it was Hannah's fault. "I can't explain it. I know I'd never feel like that in a room full of modern furniture. It just isn't the same."

She smiled. "Maybe that's why you kissed your boss. Not that you're that attracted, but maybe the furniture made you do it."

"Hannah, sometimes I don't know why I even talk to you."

She tossed her hair over her shoulder. "Because it's like talking to yourself, only better."

I shot her a look. That was usually true, but not tonight. She wasn't even trying to understand.

Hannah stood, walked to the door, and paused. "I know you're not getting attached to Ken. Since we won't be in Serendipity much longer, there's no sense in letting that happen. Just go out with him, more as a friend, because you're both single and bored, right?"

I picked at the bedspread. "Sure. Just like you're not getting attached to that cowboy neighbor of Francie's. To my knowledge, neither of us has been invited on a date by the guys we're talking about." I shot her a look she avoided. "But at this point I still work for Ken, and I want to get the place in better shape before you and I head out of town. It'll look good on my resume when I explain how I helped turn a failing business around."

It would be a major challenge, especially with Ken's hesitation to embrace change. So I'd need to do a few things without his knowing it. Once everything was in place, he couldn't help but see how brilliant my ideas were.

He'd probably try to sweep me off my feet once that

happened, but the truth was, he'd already done that without making any grand gestures. He'd done it just by being himself.

CHAPTER SIXTEEN

HANNAH AND I sat at Aunt Jacquie's dining room table, which was covered with papers. We had needed the extra space to spread everything out, picture how it would look. And since Aunt Jacquie was always interested in whatever was out of the ordinary, we'd chosen her as a confidante. Mom might have gone for it, but then again she and Dad might have insisted Ken should be in on the planning stage.

I knew Ken better than they did, and realized he wouldn't go for it. He had to be convinced by the idea's success after the fact, because he was too cautious about his store. He seemed to be trying to keep everything intact, almost like a museum. Our community had a great museum, and we didn't need another one. What Ken had wasn't working, yet he didn't acknowledge that he needed to make changes. There wasn't enough income, so he wanted to cut my hours and hope more money came in? *Hello.* It was much better to make the best possible use of the space and the—ahem—talent.

This was for Ken's own good, after all.

Jacquie brought mugs of steaming coffee and placed them at the edges of our strategic plans, then added a plate of her famous scones. Yet another reason we were smart to ask if she wanted to be part of the planning.

Our aunt's eyes sparkled with enthusiasm. "Taylor, I think you've really got a great idea. And like you said, Hannah, at first, the customers are most likely to be from out of town. But I can also see locals wanting to book a table for a special night, like an anniversary. If you get local guys educated about it, you might have some marriage proposals right there in the window of Once Upon a Time. Valentine's Day might book up weeks ahead, and with the lights on the courthouse and around the square making such a pretty setting at Christmas, that'll be busy, too."

I fidgeted in my chair. "We need customers *now*, though. The way business is running, we'll be lucky—I mean, Ken will be lucky—to keep the doors open 'til Christmas, let alone Valentine's Day."

She put a hand on my shoulder. "Calm down. I just meant those will be especially busy periods. I think once you're set up, and the word is out, you'll be surprised how popular the place becomes. Are you sure you can keep up with the food?"

I shifted again, this time not meeting her eyes. "I guess at first I might need some help. Until I find my rhythm with it, you know."

Hannah clicked a ballpoint pen open and closed. "She expects me to help, in spite of a long day at the Christmas tree farm. And we kind of think Mom will volunteer, once we tell her about it."

Jacquie laughed. "Okay, let's be realistic. Your mom will be there, and so will I. And your grandmother. I know she's in her sixties, but she can out-work a lot of women half her age. Myself included. How big did you say the kitchen is?"

I shook my head. "Tiny. Miniscule. And not well laid-out. But we can work with it." It would be a big challenge to create the meals I had in mind in that little space. "I've read that some of the best chefs actually prefer a small kitchen."

Hannah shot me a look, her brows raised. "I think you told yourself that one, Taylor. But oh well. We've got what we've got, and since good old Ken doesn't have the bucks to create something more useable..."

Jacquie looked at her. "Did you ask him, though?

Maybe you're making an inaccurate assumption."

Hannah blushed, and turned her attention to me.
"Taylor, do you want to field that one?"

Jacquie straightened, crossed her arms. "Okay, I
know there's something going on, so you'd better spill it. Is
it possible you haven't cleared any of this with Ken?"

I nodded. "More than possible. But what he doesn't
know, he can't freak out about, right? The tea room was easy
to set up. A little reorganization of the back room, and some
shifting of furniture—Okay, a lot of furniture. But still, not a
huge effort, and very worthwhile already. Yet when we first
talked about it, you'd have thought I was asking him to sever
a limb."

I pointed at the plans, the nine unique, intimate
dinner settings—three on each level, set into the windows,
with views of the courthouse square. We would seat by
reservation only, so I would know ahead of time how many
meals I was preparing. Three courses, with wine and dessert,
at a price that wasn't astronomical, yet allowed for a nice
profit. Once it caught on, like Jacquie said, it would be
popular. "I can imagine we'll have to turn people away when
the word of mouth advertising gets in gear. It's nice when
the Serendipity Gossip Tree has something positive to pass
along. Turning customers away will make them even more

determined to eat there."

Hannah was nodding, but Jacquie hadn't changed her stance since realizing Ken was oblivious to everything we'd mapped out. "Taylor, you cannot undertake this without his okay."

"He'll thank me, after. Honestly, Aunt Jacquie, if I ask him, he'll tell me *no*."

"That's his prerogative, since it's his store."

"He's going to *lose* the store. Go out of business. Don't you see? Going behind his back is the only option. This is for his own good." Ken would be devastated to get to the point where he had to shut down permanently. The fact that he was hard-headed about making any changes meant I had to take matters into my own hands. He'd eventually thank me for it.

Making the store profitable would be my gift to him. I'd come to the wrenching decision to keep our relationship platonic. Tempting as he was, falling in love with a local shopkeeper wasn't on my list of long-term goals.

She softened. "Taylor, I'm afraid you're too close to see the situation clearly. However, I can understand dealing with a man who finds change difficult. And I know a lot of local stores have been struggling. From what I hear, the store wasn't doing well a long time before Mr. Hendrickson died.

I'll help you with this, because, like you, I think it will do Ken good. I think, too, the community will benefit."

Whew. There for a minute I thought she was going to bail. I held up my hand and she high-fived me.

"Once Upon a Time won't know what hit it," Hannah said.

"And neither will Ken," Jacquie agreed.

I hoped it wasn't going to be as ominous as they made it sound.

CHAPTER SEVENTEEN

ABOUT ONCE A month, Ken changed the first-floor window displays. So when I suggested creating three intimate dining spaces with the stuff we had on hand, he wasn't too hard to convince. The second and third floors, however, required more talking.

"I don't understand why you're suddenly so obsessed with tables for two," he complained.

"You said changing the windows is one way to bring people in."

"Yes, I said that, but to be honest I'm not sure I believe it. Hasn't done much good so far."

"Ah, but now we'll have a uniform look for the whole front of the store."

He smirked. "How many people will even notice that?"

"I don't know that very many will *consciously* notice

it, but subconsciously, we'll be going from clutter to class."
The phrase had popped out of my mouth on its own volition,
but I liked the sound of it.

Ken seemed to like it, too. He helped me move a
small round oak table into a second-floor window, and
considered. "I want to say it's nonsense, but maybe you're
right. Plus, we're not out anything for trying. But if you
decide to move it all again a month from now, at that point I
may not go along with it."

If all went well, a month from now I wouldn't be
around here anymore, but I didn't want to put that damper on
the afternoon. He was frowning though, so maybe the
thought had occurred to him. We hadn't said anything yet
about the kiss. I dreaded having to break the news that we
needed to be just friends.

"Taylor, having you here has made a huge
difference."

A stupid blush hit my face. "Yeah? I think that
might be a compliment."

He nodded, setting the chairs in place and standing
back while I added a white cloth, a hand-painted ceramic
flower vase, and two cut-glass candlestick holders. Each
little dining nook would be unique. Each item had a tag on it,
so if a diner actually wanted to buy something, we'd know

which account got the money.

As we moved to the next window and started the process again, he cleared his throat, and eventually spoke, his voice soft. "About that night, when we were setting up the tea room. That shouldn't have happened. My fault. And it won't happen again."

I jerked my attention away from the work at hand. The work I was doing for him, though he didn't know that yet. He looked miserable, obviously regretting that moment that transformed us from boss and employee to just man and woman. I had known it was a mistake then, had told myself a thousand times not to read anything into my attraction and his response.

I was lucky that he was saying this, so I didn't have to be the bad guy and do the *just friends* speech. I should feel relieved, not hurt. Maybe, in time, I would.

I shrugged, hoping I looked nonchalant. "No big deal, Ken. It was a long day, and we were both tired. Plus, the romantic lighting. See how right I was to suggest a chandelier?"

His laugh was bigger than the weak joke deserved, and I knew he was relieved I had given him an easy out. We created the rest of the romantic dining nooks with very little conversation, none of which was personal. I told myself that was a good thing, because once this little venture was a success, and I had it duly noted on an updated resume and uploaded online everywhere, I expected to shake the dust of Serendipity off my feet.

Including the dust I kept flicking off antiques every single day, for a man who didn't know a good thing when he saw it.

CHAPTER EIGHTEEN

KEN DIDN'T FIGURE out what was going on until the first couple arrived for dinner. They were tiny cabin B&B guests that Francie had steered our way.

Even though it was almost closing time, Ken greeted them like he did everyone else. "Hello. How may we help you today?"

The couple smiled, looking at each other like they were star-struck in love. I thought I might gag.

"We're here for dinner," the woman said, putting an arm through her husband's. "Grier, table for two?"

The look on Ken's face was priceless. "You— dinner? Sorry, but you've got the wrong place. You must be looking for—"

I almost knocked into him in my rush to greet them. "Me! They're looking for me, because I've got their table set up, and a fabulous dinner planned." Ken stood immobile, mouth open, and I led them to the third floor. They seemed agile enough, and it would put distance between them and Ken while I got him calmed down.

"That man downstairs..." Mr. Grier started, but let the sentence trail off.

"Don't mind Ken. He hasn't seen the guest list yet. I'll go take care of that, and be right back with your salads. Thank you so much for dining with us."

Mrs. Grier reached across the table and took her husband's hand. "When Francie told us about it, I couldn't miss the chance. I think you're smart to have guests choose their meals ahead of time, but I haven't seen that done before."

I couldn't help the laugh. "If you saw the size of our kitchen, you'd understand why we're doing it that way. Anyway, super glad to have you, and I'll be right back."

They relaxed into their chairs, having just discovered the view of the majestic castle-like courthouse. "No rush," said Mr. Grier. "We're here to enjoy."

Thank goodness that was the outlook of the other diners, too. Since we only had three couples tonight, I thought it best to put one on each floor, allowing plenty of privacy for conversation. I wondered how great it looked from outside. That was more free advertising.

Spreading everyone out made lots of exercise for me, and I was thankful for the old pulley-style elevator. I put the food for floors two and three on it, pulled it up to three, gave them their meals, then sent it down to two and did the same. Hannah was good help in the kitchen. With such a small first night the two of us could handle easily handle it alone. When Ken was on board and we were busier, I'd talk to Mom and Gran about helping.

Speaking of alone, I hadn't seen Ken since the Griers arrived. I had rehearsed what I would say to him, the answers to any and all arguments he could come up with. But his disappearance bothered me more than a confrontation would have.

When I said good night to the last of the three couples, and saw them get into their vehicle and start it, I locked the door and turned off the outside light. Hannah was almost done washing dishes. "You do good work," I said, picking up a towel and drying.

"Remember, you're not going to have me forever."

"How about if I let you be the hostess next time? That's kind of fun. I don't mind doing the kitchen."

She tipped her head, considering. "Hmm. Maybe. So, I have never seen your boss. When I arrived, you sneaked me back here so fast I didn't get a glimpse. I wanted to see how he reacted to your takeover."

I thought of the nice amount of money the night had brought in, even subtracting the cost of the food and wine. "Don't call it a takeover. That sounds negative."

Ken appeared in the doorway, his face looking like a spring storm. "Negative? That's putting it lightly." Then he registered Hannah's presence, and like most people who see us together for the first time, he was confused, looking from one of us to the other. "Taylor," he said to me, "we need to talk."

Now, *that* sounded negative.

****

Hannah and I finished the dishes and put them away, while Ken stalked around like a caged lion, occasionally glaring at me.

Finally, she and I headed to the door. "Well, we're done, so we'll be going," I said in Ken's direction with false cheer in my voice.

He planted himself between us and the exit. "I need for you to stay, Taylor."

I smiled sweetly up at him. "But Hannah's my ride. We share a car, remember?"

"Yes, I do. I also remember that this is *my* store, not

yours. And that never once did you mention that you wanted to serve dinner in those little alcoves we set up."

Hannah clapped her hands together. "So, I'm out of here. Heading to DQ for a snack, and I'll be back in"—she looked at Ken—"half an hour?"

He nodded, and she fled. *Coward.* It wasn't her fight, so I shouldn't really blame her. But why did it have to be a fight at all? Here I was, doing Ken a big favor again, like I had with the tea room, and he was being a jerk about it.

He crooked his finger after locking the door, and we sat in one of the alcoves on the first floor. Cars and pickup trucks drove around the square in the near-dark, and the courthouse looked impressive as always. The antique-looking street lights added to the perfection of the scene. What a lovely spot to have a relaxing, delicious meal and a glass of wine with someone you loved.

But the closest to that I had was Ken, who was attractive, and I liked him a lot, especially when he wasn't being a butt-head. But I couldn't love him, because... My mind searched for the reasons I came up with after the kiss that shouldn't have happened.

I shook my head, to bring it back to the conversation at hand, instead of the one in my head. "Wow, I haven't sat in any of these little alcoves. It really is a neat feeling." I moved my eyes to Ken. "Isn't it?"

He glowered. "Don't look so pleased with yourself. I am absolutely livid about this, Taylor."

I slid the delicate vase around on the linen cloth. "Livid? That means really mad, right?"

His frown deepened. "Yes. I should have known you were up to something major back when you suggested the license to sell alcohol."

"Besides the dinners, there could be some really popular book club events. Wine and books. That's a nice combo. We might talk it up..."

"Don't go off on another tangent when we haven't dealt with this one yet. You went behind my back, advertised my place of business as a restaurant. Do you realize we can't legally serve wine? You did all this behind my back, and I've been made to look like a fool."

Now we'd reached the real problem. "That's it, isn't it? Not that I came up with a great idea, and already the first night we've netted more than some *weeks* I've worked here. What bothers you is that Mr. and Mrs. Grier, who live who-knows-where and will never meet you again, thought you were clueless."

"Because I *was* clueless. Because you made me clueless."

"No, that happened a long time ago. I just kept you in the dark. That's a different thing." *Oops. Flippant attitude might not be my best tactic here.*

"Taylor..." His composure was slipping. I didn't fear him physically, because I knew him better than to anticipate that kind of reaction. But I was worried that he didn't seem to be coming around yet.

"Ken. This is a *money maker.* You don't have to close the store, you don't have to get a job to support the store, or whatever other ridiculous thing you might do because you're so sentimental about this place. Now that you see the possibilities, you can jump through the hoops to get a license for serving wine, and it's all good."

His face kept getting redder, and I hurried on. "Listen, I get that you loved your uncle and want to honor his memory. But honestly, letting the place sit here, making little to no profit, makes zero sense. I can't afford to work for free. I need a job that brings me an income, and most people are like that. Your attitude about your uncle's business makes no sense at all. You've got something here. Not a goldmine, but it has possibilities. With the tea room and now the fine dining, we're edging toward making it a success."

He clapped his hands over his ears, and in a moment

removed them slowly, shaking his head. "You're fired."

What? I couldn't believe it. I had expected anger, aggravation. But losing my job when I was trying to do him this big favor?

I guess I didn't say anything, because he repeated it. "You're fired, Taylor. And I think your sister is pulling up outside."

I saw the headlights swing toward us, bathing us in their garish glow.

Ken rose and unlocked the door, held it for me. "Good-bye."

I'm not often at a loss for words. But the unfairness of this situation, when I had done so much to make his business a success, hit me hard. I hitched up my handbag and squared my shoulders, marched to the car, and slammed the door after I was in.

Hannah knew things were bad. "Seat belt," she whispered, backing out and pulling into traffic.

I didn't look to see if Ken was watching us. I would never look for him again.

****

The parents were immediately on my case to find another job, and worse than that, they took Ken's side.

"What were you thinking, Taylor?" Dad asked while Mom made that irritating *tsk-ing* sound. "Making him look like a fool is one thing, but taking his business in a direction he wasn't even aware of?" He waved his hands, not knowing what else to say.

Thank goodness.

But Mom continued the rant. "Taylor, Ken is a friend of ours. I feel badly, as if your father and I have somehow betrayed him."

"Mom, get a grip. You didn't know about it." I felt like screaming at how unfair everyone was being. "I keep waiting for anyone to acknowledge that what I did was for Ken's sake. It's not like I wanted to stay there long-term. I was just creating a way for him to keep the store. I think it was kind of ingenious."

"That may be, dear, but..." Mom shrugged, losing momentum. "Well, it's done now. I hope you've learned that making unilateral decisions on matters of importance is a sure way to kill a relationship."

Her soft voice got through to me more than Dad's anger, and some of what they said finally made sense. I had tried to do something wonderful for Ken, but had gone about it all wrong. My heart was pounding when I muttered, "We didn't have a relationship."

She put an arm around my shoulders. "Well, you're certainly not going to now."

Alone in my room, I pulled out one of Opal's diaries, and turned to a passage I'd read many times, and had marked with a slip of paper. Hey, I was already down— might as well wallow.

When I see him, my heart flutters. When we part, for even a short while, I feel as if my life is over. He has the power to light my day, or plunge me into deepest despair. Love is the most wonderful, terrible feeling in the world.

Sing it, sister. Sing it.

CHAPTER NINETEEN

OUT OF THE blue, I got an interview request through one of my online postings.

Hannah was more excited than I was. "Now, see? It's a good thing you got fired. Now you have a chance at a job that matters."

"It means commuting to Louisville every day. You need to get a job in that area too, remember." Her excitement waned quickly as I spoke. "We're going to rent an apartment together in the city. Is any of this sounding familiar, Hannah?"

She shrugged, looking sheepish.

"Oh, do *not* tell me you're seriously considering hanging around Serendipity because of that cowboy." I'd seen the guy from a distance. Sure, he was rugged and cute, but she and I had plans, and the guy hadn't made a single move to even ask her out.

"I dunno," she said. "I'm confused right now. Plus Francie needs me. One of the others on our crew quit, to work in the factory. I couldn't leave right now, Taylor. It wouldn't be fair to her."

I sat back, arms crossed over my chest. "Okay. I get that. But you are still submitting online applications, right?"

Hannah looked away, played with the ends of her hair. Bad sign. Everything about this cowboy was wrong for my sister, but if I tried to convince her of that, she'd be mad at me, and twice as crazy about him.

****

I pulled out my interview suit. It had been cleaned and pressed since last time I wore it, traipsing around the town square, and then all over three levels of Ken's store. How long ago that day seemed. And how messed up, that a job I didn't want in the first place had turned into something interesting and challenging. And the boss who'd been so stand-offish was now the man I was trying not to mourn, as half of an almost-relationship.

The truth was, I didn't want a job in Louisville. Not even if Hannah got one too, and we could share a cute apartment, starting to live out the dreams we'd talked about so many times.

Instead of that dream, I wanted the one in Serendipity, and its name was Ken Abernathy. Was there any way he and I could patch things up, give each other a new start? I kept quiet about these thoughts. I'd given Hannah a rough way to go for staying at the tree farm and mooning about her cowboy. I didn't dare tell her I felt the same way about my favorite antiques store owner.

I had to go to the interview, because the whole family knew I'd received the contact. There had been no other topic of conversation last night at the dinner table. I couldn't mope around about Ken, and had no idea how to get him to give a second chance to the possibility of our relationship.

I'd started working at Once Upon a Time in early May, and now it was mid-July. The humidity was oppressive, and made my hair curl even more than usual. The heat made my suit ridiculous, but I didn't have anything appropriate that would be comfortable. Nothing was comfortable in mid-July in Southern Indiana, except air conditioning.

The drive to the east side of Louisville wasn't bad, since our car's A/C was working great. I'd done the route a million times to hit a mall, or out to a movie or dinner. I'd heard of some employers choosing to do first interviews in public places, to see how the prospective candidate functioned in a social atmosphere, surrounded by distractions. So I hadn't been too surprised that I was meeting the interviewer at a coffee, salad, and sandwich shop.

Even if I didn't get the job, I'd have lunch and a cup of decent caffeine. I found a parking space, smoothed the skirt of my suit, and put on the jacket in spite of the heat. I'd pulled my hair up into a no-nonsense chignon, and sprayed the heck out of it, hoping to look serious, and maybe a year or two older.

During the drive, a plan started to form in my mind. I'd do my worst at this interview, and then drive straight back to Serendipity, walk into Once Upon a Time, and demand my job back. Well, maybe it wasn't a great plan, but the first part, throwing the interview, was definitely a winner. I would work out the second part on the road home.

But when I saw the guy I was here to meet, everything about my plans for the interview went out of my head. My mental review of Interviewing Skills 101 all went out the window.

Because the guy I was here to meet turned out to be Ken. He was wearing his usual—black jeans and shirt. The snug fit of the shirt made me think of the muscles under it. I pushed the memory of our kiss out of my head, at least mostly.

Ken rose when he saw me, and his chair nearly toppled over. Catching it, his smile faltered, then revived.

I don't know if I had a smile or just a look of pure shock. "Ken? You posted an online opening? You tricked me into coming down here?"

He nodded. "The truth is, I have a business that needs the touch of someone who isn't afraid to take chances."

I regarded him for a moment before pulling out a chair and sitting down across from him. I wished for a cup of coffee right now, to help me better grasp what he was saying. "I thought you *didn't* want someone like that."

He nodded. "That's what I thought, too. Um, let me buy your lunch, okay?"

At least I'd get a free meal out of it. That wouldn't make up for wearing this hot suit and heels when the temp outside felt like 110. It wouldn't make up for a lot of things. But still, might as well enjoy. I gave him my order and sat there, letting him take care of it. It felt good to let Ken do *my* bidding for a change. I didn't want to get my hopes up too high, though.

When he returned to the table with the food, he said,

"Taylor, I wanted us to both get out of town, so we could have a private discussion."

I glanced around at the crowd. "This place is full of people."

He nodded. "People who don't know either of us, our families, or our stories."

I picked up my fork and started on my salad, hoping I wouldn't make a mess on the skirt and have to pay for it to be dry-cleaned again. "Putting it that way, you're right. It's pretty private."

"Let me try to explain my situation, and then we can see where we go from here."

That sounded promising. "Okay."

He took a deep breath, looking miserable. "Uncle Jay left the store to my grandmother, who is his sister. She's in her eighties, and couldn't manage it. Yet she would have been heartbroken to sell it, because he had loved it so, and loved Serendipity. So she handed it over to me. She insisted on selling it to me for one dollar, saying she trusted me. It would have been easier if she had laid down some hard and fast tenets, but she trusted me with this dream of her brother's. I've told you what a wonderful man he was. Very generous with his time, and with his love."

He sounded like a great guy, and I was sorry I'd

never taken the time to get to know him. "Was he married? I don't remember a Mrs. Hendrickson."

"No, he never married. He got close once, but the unthinkable happened. Yet he never gave up on love. He told me once that whenever I met the girl of my dreams, I was to stick with her, no matter what."

My breath caught at the way his eyes held mine. Then he looked down at his hands, tightly holding a cardboard coffee mug I hoped was up to the test.

"Her request, that I take the store, came at the perfect moment. I'd just escaped a disastrous relationship with a woman who was both my fiancée, and my business partner. She made a lot of unilateral decisions, taking the business in a direction I didn't approve of. I broke our engagement, and let her buy out my part of the business. I vowed never to let that happen again."

Ouch. "Never to...get engaged, or have a business partner?"

His eyes were intense. "Both, really. And definitely not be engaged to a business partner, or let that partner make decisions I wasn't part of. Can you see why I was so upset at what you did?"

I'd told myself I needed to apologize to Ken, and I wasn't going to try to defend myself—at least, not too much.

"Yes, I see, sort of. But—can I just say that it looked like you were losing your shirt on the place? I don't know, maybe you're a millionaire from that business deal with your ex, and don't need money, but most people are in business to make a profit. I was trying to help you. Can you see that?"

He held up his hands. "Here's how it felt to me. That you were trying to change everything. The fact that you went behind my back—that was unconscionable."

If I was going to be around him, I needed to start doing that word test in *Readers Digest.* "Does that mean it was really bad?"

He sighed. "Close enough."

"But if I did a bad thing, trying to do a very good thing, like keep you in business?" I shut my mouth, took a deep breath. "Listen, I told myself I needed to apologize to you, and that I wouldn't try to get you to see things my way. So here goes—I realize I should have asked before setting up the dinners. And I should have found out about licenses and stuff. But I was afraid you wouldn't see the potential, and would shoot it down without giving it a chance."

"Which is basically what I did, I suppose. You might be interested to know that I've taken the first steps to get the store cleared for serving food and wine *legally.*"

"Yes. But I—" I closed my mouth, realizing he

wasn't disagreeing with me. "You did?"

He smiled, nodding. "Taylor, could you see your way clear to give me another chance? I've called myself every kind of fool for letting you go. Uncle Jay told me not to do that, you see."

EPILOGUE

I SIGHED, LIGHTLY touching the lovely gown hanging in the wardrobe. It was perfect, just the way I had hoped it would look. My heart fluttered as I imagined the moment I started down the aisle toward him. Encouraged by the reassurance in his smile, I would overcome my shyness at being the focus of all attention. His eyes would shine with love, and he would reach out his hand to me. At last, we would become husband and wife.

Arrangements had been made for family and friends to be in attendance for the joining of my life to my beloved's. Why then did I have this tug of concern that something was wrong? I shook my head to dislodge the worries. Just a short time more to wait. Nothing could go amiss.

****

I jumped when the door opened.

Hannah rolled her eyes, stepped in, and closed the door quietly behind her. "It's just me, silly."

Hannah was still in her robe too. So that was good. My hand shook slightly, as I picked up the tiny silver antique clock from the bedside table. Yes, there was time. No reason to rush around to get dressed. I glanced toward the closet where my wedding gown was hanging...well, not my gown exactly, but the one I was going to wear.

Hannah planted herself in front of me, leaned over and looked into my eyes. "Wow, Taylor, you're a bundle of nerves. It's not too late to back out if you're having second thoughts."

I leapt off my bed. Turning away from her, I walked to the window and stared out at the backyard.

"Why would you say something like that? Of course I'm not having second thoughts. Ken is the love of my life."

Hannah put an arm around my shoulders. "I know that. And you know that. And, like, today is supposed to be *happy* because of it, right? So lighten up."

"How can I lighten up when I've—Oh Hannah, you don't understand."

"Understand what?"

"I'm worried about my dress. I mean, it's kind of

154

unexpected, isn't it?"

She let out a long breath. "Oh, there's a novel thought. The woman who fell in love with her boss love at first sight, nearly drove him away trying to fix his business, and when he finally woke up and proposed, insisted she didn't want the typical Kincaid church wedding, or to even try for a Carla Standish gown? It will be a surprise to anybody that *that* woman has done something unexpected?"

"Well, since you put it that way... I just can't help wondering how people will take it. Not that I'm really questioning myself."

Hannah crossed her arms. "Sure sounds like you are."

"Not exactly. I mean, I've always had this feeling, you know?"

She nodded. "You and your trunk. I hope the two of you will be very happy together."

I laughed. "Thanks. I needed some levity added to my day."

Hannah winked. "No problem. And in spite of the unusual—or, hey maybe because of it—I think this will be a lovely wedding. We've got a stunning bride, handsome groom, the whole family assembled in our parents' backyard, and a beautiful day to do the deed. What could be better?"

I hugged her tightly. I knew down deep that wearing Opal's dress, and having the wedding in the yard where she wanted to marry her beloved Jeremiah, was the right thing to do, for me, and for Opal. Still, I was glad to have Hannah's reassurance. I released her, not wanting to start tears for either of us.

"For what it's worth, Taylor, I think this is going to be wonderful. You're giving Opal her chance at last."

I nodded, feeling a rush of enthusiasm again. "Exactly. That's how it feels to me."

With an arm around Hannah's shoulders, I pulled her to the mirror. "We could pay ten times as much to get our hair done in the city."

She put up a tentative hand to her head full of complicated braids, twists and swirls. It was understated from a distance, but up close one could see the detail. It had taken ages, at a shop at the edge of the Serendipity city limits.

Part of the time I sat watching Hannah's being created, I had been thinking of Opal. She and her sister had planned to wear their long, dark hair up, too.

My hairdo was similar to Hannah's but even more intricate, with strings of narrow white tatting and "pearl" beads worked into it, too. It would be amazing with the dress and simple veil. Now I studied my reflection. "I just hope it will come down without too much trouble."

Hannah smiled. "I'm sure Ken is talented enough to dismantle your hairstyle, Taylor. But hey—first things first. Try not to think too much about the honeymoon. Your face is turning red."

Thoughts of the honeymoon weren't causing my blush. Well, not entirely, at least. Yes, I could imagine Ken would enjoy the challenge of taking my hair down. He would do it slowly, with amazing kisses, and caresses in all the right places. My face got hotter.

Hannah was right, it was a mistake to anticipate that already. Between now and then there were other things to navigate. Specifically the wedding, and at the reception, inevitable questions about my gown.

I wouldn't lie. Lying would be dishonest, and unfair to Opal, and this day was partly for her. Our wedding guests would be sure the rest of Serendipity heard about Opal's gown by the end of the day. Of that I had no doubt.

Mom opened the door, dressed in ice blue and looking fabulous. "Girls, it's time." She swept into the room, and helped me into the amazingly sexy dress that had been waiting in the trunk all these years. The satin was form-fitting, with a wide neckline and skinny straps. Every curve of my body was outlined by the simple, elegant gown. Then she attached the close-fitting white wreath into my hair, the way the stylist had demonstrated earlier in the day.

When Hannah was zipped into her gown, they both helped attach Opal's floor-skimming tulle veil to the wreath in my hair.

Mom made sure everything was just right, as she had always done for us.

I hugged her. "I love you, Mom."

"I know, honey. And I love you. I'm proud of you, Taylor, for standing up for what's right. For knowing love when you found it, and for being true to it, and to Ken."

We picked up the bouquets of old-fashioned flowers, created to resemble the ones Opal had planned in her diary. Then we waited for our cue.

****

Ken and his best man, a college roommate and best friend whom I'd met a few times, had dressed downstairs, in the little room Emily had lived in before marrying David. When the church organist started playing the intro music on our piano, which had been pushed up near the open living room window, Mom gave us both air kisses and hurried downstairs. She, Gran, and Ken's mother, Crystal, would be seated by our brother Ben and Aunt Jacquie's husband Nick, who were ushers. I was so sorry that his grandmother wasn't well enough to attend.

I had fleetingly thought of asking Emily if Isabel could be a flower girl, but decided to stick with the simple plan, more like Opal had outlined.

The next song started, which meant Ken and his best man were moving into place, along with our preacher, Reverend Bobby. Hannah and I went downstairs, and waited at the back door, where Dad was standing.

Hannah slow-stepped down the aisle, looking cool and lovely. Her cowboy wasn't here, and I was unclear where that relationship might be headed.

Once she was in place near the preacher, the music changed again. The wedding march began, and my heart thumped along with it. Dad, resplendent in his black tux, took my arm, smiled his good George Clooney smile, and we headed into the yard, toward Ken, and my future. When we came into sight, Mom stood up, and everyone else followed suit. Gran and Aunt Jacquie gave me thumbs-up when we passed.

A light breeze played with the long, diaphanous veil. Part of my brain heard sounds like *ooh* and *aah* during the walk down the grassy aisle. I stopped near enough to Ken that I could feel the heat of his body. Could he smell the old-fashioned scent I'd used this morning? I couldn't—was barely breathing at this point.

Somehow we got through the parts of the ceremony that required us to move or say something. I wasn't sure how that happened, but finally Reverend Bobby announced that we were man and wife. Ken was invited to kiss his bride.

He took me in his arms, one hand holding my waist while the other slid up my back to my nearly-bare shoulders. The kiss may have lasted a moment longer than was expected, but to me—to us—it wasn't even a beginning.

Happy tears burned at the back of my eyes as the kiss ended. Ken's look promised infinitely more, once we were alone. I grinned up at him when he pulled me close for another brief kiss, sealing the agreement.

We walked slowly back down the aisle, letting anyone take pictures if they wished, saying a few words to those in the aisle seats. Instead of a receiving line, we went directly to the big white tent where the food would be served.

Ken glanced down at me. His eyes rested for a moment on the delicate silver locket I wore on a long chain around my neck. "Your dress is perfect, Taylor." He slid his hand around my waist again. "Where did you find it?"

"In the attic. Pretty cool, huh?"

He laughed, then saw I wasn't kidding. "There's a bridal shop called The Attic?"

"No, there's an attic." I pointed to the top of the house. "I found this dress, the veil, and shoes in a trunk years ago when we were kids. I was always enthralled with it."

Ken took a step back and did another head to toe appraisal. "Wow. The dress could have been made for you."

"Yep. I sort of grew into it."

His gaze grew hot. "Something for which I will be thankful every day of my life." He kissed me again, slowly and thoroughly.

The guests were pouring into the tent now, too. Ken's mother, Crystal Abernathy, hurried over to us, embracing us both in turn.

"What a beautiful wedding. I don't know when I've seen a more perfect setting for an outdoor event, and such a lovely crowd. And Taylor—that dress is simply divine. Wherever did you find it?"

I looked at Ken and then back to my mother-in-law. "Crystal, it's kind of a funny story."

"We're all ears," said Crystal, gesturing at the gathering throng.

Hannah appeared and put her arm through mine. "Hey, guys, you're supposed to be up there with the microphone if you're going to say anything interesting."

She nudged us further into the tent, to the head table where the wedding party and our parents would sit. We all stood at the spots indicated by our place cards, still chatting among ourselves. Eventually Mom and Dad, hand in hand, made their way through the happy crowd and found their spots too. Dad tapped a spoon on the side of a wineglass, but the gentle ringing didn't faze the guests. So Aunt Jacquie put two fingers in her mouth and whistled shrilly through her teeth. Everyone quieted down, and Dad stepped to the mic.

Speeches were made, toasts drunk. A large amount of delicious food was consumed, thanks to the catering expertise of the good folks at Chez Gwen. The cake, created by Something Sweet, was tall but simple—an art deco type design. I had found a photo on Pinterest that suited the look I was trying to achieve. I'd had to explain to the baker that yes, I did want a cake that looked appropriate for a wedding in the 1930s.

I knew there was probably talk behind my back about that. The napkins had an art deco-inspired edge, and *Taylor & Ken* and the date in one corner. Everything about the reception, and even the bouquets Hannah and I had carried, would have looked appropriate to a wedding held in that time period. I had explained repeatedly that I wanted everything to coordinate with my dress. But it was more than that. Today was for me and Ken, but it was also for Opal.

Opal had hoped for a beautiful wedding, the start of her life with her beloved Jeremiah. Through her diaries, I had followed their romance. I'd even vicariously lived through the creation of the gown and veil by Opal's mother who was an exquisitely talented seamstress. The white leather shoes had arrived by mail through the Montgomery Ward catalog. All the plans were set for the wedding on the lawn of the house Opal's parents had built. The house that I grew up in.

Three weeks before the wedding date, the diary ended.

When Ken had proposed to me, I was ecstatic. Though I didn't tell him why, I felt compelled to somehow honor Opal in the wedding plans. I tried on the dress after years of admiring it, and found that it fit me perfectly. The shoes were tight, but they were leather, and I could stretch them out a bit. I'd put on the veil too, and looking in a mirror, saw myself—but also a shadow of something else. A dream unfulfilled—Opal's dream.

Ken never questioned my desire to give our wedding

a subtle 1930s theme. Hannah, knowing how much the trunk full of treasures had always meant to me, willingly found a straight, silky gown in oyster pink that complemented my— Opal's—gown perfectly.

Crystal leaned over the table to catch my eye. "Your mother tells me there's a story behind your beautiful gown. I'd love to hear it."

I related what I knew of the tale of Opal and Jeremiah, watching Crystal's reaction but especially Ken's. He seemed to grow more interested with each word.

"What was Jeremiah's last name?" Ken asked when I finished.

"Um. I don't know, except that it began with an *H*. There was some kind of superstition that if she wrote his last name, she'd never marry him."

"Hendrickson," Ken said.

I didn't know, but was getting tingles all over about this conversation. "Maybe. But—that's your uncle's last name."

Crystal's face was flushed with excitement. "Yes, exactly. My mother's brother was Jeremiah Hendrickson. He moved to Serendipity, bought that big building on the town square, planning to run a furniture shop with his wife-to-be."

Ken whirled to look at her. "Mom, remember how

Uncle Jay talked about Opal, how much he'd loved her, how beautiful she was?" He looked at me then, his eyes bright—with unshed tears? "And that she had died right before their wedding was to take place?"

My breath caught. She died? Jeremiah didn't abandon her? "But—Jeremiah—"

Ken explained, "When I was a little guy, I couldn't say his whole name. It was a mouthful. So he told me to just use the first letter. Uncle J."

He squeezed my hand. "He loved her so much, he never married. But oh, how he talked about her." Ken pulled a pocket watch from his vest. "He gave this to me, because I always loved to listen to his stories. He said he wanted me to have the watch to remind me that whenever I met the girl of my dreams, I was to stick with her, no matter what."

I smiled. He had told me his uncle's advice once before. "But how can a watch remind you of that?"

"Not the watch as much as the picture inside." He pushed the button and the cover opened, revealing the watch face on one side, and on the other, a tiny photograph of a young couple.

The world seemed to come to a skidding halt.

"Opal," I whispered. My shaking hands reached to the delicate silver locket around my neck. It took me a couple of tries to open it, but there inside was the same photo.

Jeremiah and Opal had finally gone down the aisle, on the lawn of the big house just as they'd planned. As Opal's mother had promised her, the dress had received rave reviews.

And Ken and I realized, even more than we already had, that with enough effort, love truly could last forever.

The End

...or is it The Beginning?

A NOTE FROM THE AUTHOR

Thank you so very much for reading Taylor and Ken's book!

Years ago, I wrote the wedding scene as a short story, but chose not to publish it. I'm so glad to be able to provide this happy ending for two generations of Serendipity characters in ONCE UPON A TIME.

When Taylor and Hannah popped onto the page as wrote EMILY'S DREAMS, I didn't have plans for their future. But by the end of Emily's story, when she had undergone such a transformation, I knew I wanted to give her younger sisters a chance to redeem themselves, too.

I started writing this book, not knowing who the hero would be until the wind caught those papers and Ken Abernathy opened the door of the antiques store. My stories don't always unfold that way, but it's much more fun when they do. I hope the story was as much fun for you to read!

I'm sure you got the hints that Hannah is going to have a romance of her own. Look for A COWBOY FOR CHRISTMAS in Autumn 2017.

I always love to hear from readers. You can email me through the contact box on my website: http://www.magdalenascott.com.

I also send a monthly-*ish* newsletter. To sign up for that, enter your email in the form on this page: http://www.magdalenascott.com/p/contact.html

Until we meet again—Happy Reading!

Magdalena

OTHER BOOKS IN THE SERENDIPITY, INDIANA SERIES

SMALL TOWN CHRISTMAS

Melissa is moving back to Serendipity, Indiana to raise her young son and run her new business—in spite of a painful past and the fact that her ex-boyfriend still lives in their hometown.

EMILY'S DREAMS

Emily Kincaid has a second chance at life, and a voice in her head that keeps nudging her along. But she can't move forward without dealing with her past.

CHRISTMAS WEDDING

Dec. 1: Jim Standish is ready, right this minute, to marry the love of his life, but Melissa Singer wants the day to be one they'll look back on forever. Planning and execution time: 25 days. Is it possible to create the perfect Christmas Wedding?

THE BLANK BOOK

Alice Williams is surviving widowhood, but must unlock the secrets of a mysterious blank book before she can confidently step into her future with a man she's afraid to love.

THE RING

Carla Standish's life and career are going according to plan, until the rainy day in Dublin when an elderly gentleman hands her an antique Claddagh ring...

THE ROAD NOT TAKEN

Francie Standish Carrington and husband Brad are spending Christmas in her hometown of Serendipity, but it's no vacation. There are marital problems, career decisions, and a major change on the horizon for the Standish family Christmas tree farm. Can Francie find a way through all this, to a happy ending for anyone?

A PIECE OF HER SOUL

Nick Marshall has a hole in his soul, and Jacqueline must help him find the missing piece. Their teenage history in the gossipy town of Serendipity compounds the situation, as Jacqueline's visit to help her injured mother (Reba Markland, EMILY'S DREAMS) turns into something more.

ONCE UPON A TIME

Taylor Kincaid has big plans for her life, and falling in love with the mysterious new shop owner in her hometown isn't one of them. Sweet romance, "coincidences" that might be more than that, and a love that survives the unthinkable come together in this new Serendipity, Indiana tale.

A COWBOY FOR CHRISTMAS

Hannah Kincaid has her eye on the new dude ranch's head honcho, Jacob Hollingsworth, and nobody in Serendipity can predict what will happen next. Least of all them!

****

KIM: BEACH BRIDES SERIES

Jon Whitfield was engaged when he "landed" the message in a bottle on a fishing trip, and it disappeared before he could decide whether to respond. Now unattached, he's on a road trip with Kim Rose, whose gratitude in spite of a painful past reminds him of the touching note he wishes he'd kept.

Pssst--Serendipity readers, Kim was the nurse aid in Serendipity, Indiana Book 2, Emily's Dreams!

THE MCCLAINS OF LEGEND, TENNESSEE SERIES

MIDNIGHT IN LEGEND, TN

CHRISTMAS COLLISION

WHERE HER HEART IS

BUILDING A DREAM

SECOND CHANCES

CHRISTMAS CHARM

UNDER THE MISTLETOE (Prequel)

THE HOLLY AND THE IVY (Prequel)

For Free Reads, Sneak Previews & backstage info, become a Newsletter Subscriber!

My Newsletter Subscribers are Awesome!

I love to connect with readers! Please sign up for my newsletter so we can stay in touch. Don't worry about me clogging up your email inbox—I only send an email if I have actual news to share. The sign-up form is on my website:
http://www.magdalenascott.com/p/contact.html